I0575232

Jenifer Wood

Cover Illustration by Chocological.Art.

Cover design by Ash Raven.

Editing by Alex Yuschik and Emily Michel.

No part of this book was created using AI (Artificial Intelligence)

Welcome to scenic HALLOW'S COVE

Hallow's Cove is a charming small town at the juncture of mountain and sea, originally founded nearly a century ago as a refuge for the supernatural. Now occupied primarily by monsters, Hallow's Cove has become a destination for tourists of all kinds who seek to enjoy hiking, skiing, swimming, and more. Visit at any time of year to experience this quaint, old-fashioned town and all the fun activities and natural beauty it has to offer!

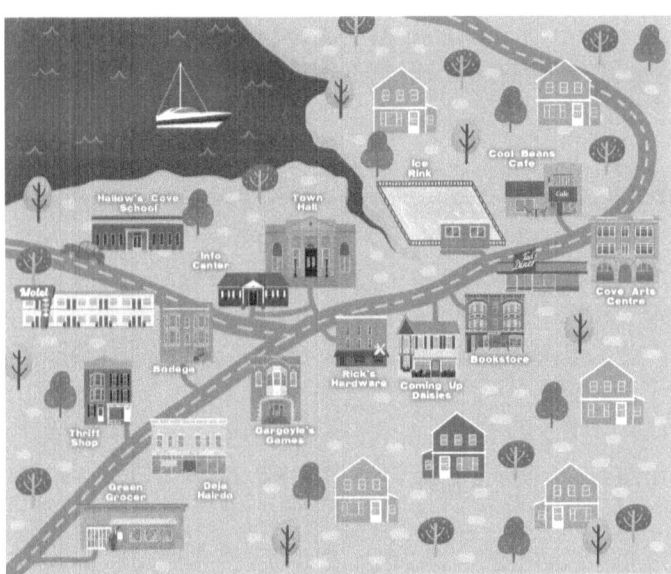

Story Introduction

LEA THOMSON ARRIVES IN the charming town of Hallows Cove with plans to open a second location of her family's flower shop, seeking a fresh start after the devastating loss of her mother. Staying at the local inn, she scopes out the dilapidated shop she's purchased sight unseen, planning to stay under the radar until she's ready for her grand opening. But then she runs into Rick, a handsome minotaur, and sparks immediately fly.

But Rick has never had a serious relationship and likes to play it "casual." Thinking Lea isn't going to stick around, he leaves the next morning without even saying goodbye. When he discovers it's going to be Lea's flower shop beside his hardware store, an ugly confrontation sets the two at odds before renovation has even begun. Can Lea and Rick get past their troubled beginnings to embrace the undeniable attraction between them?

Content Warnings

- Parental death (past)

- Rough sex (consensual)

- Alcohol use (drunkenness)

Chapter One

Lea

My shears hovered over the plant in front of me, but my mind wasn't on the task of making the sad rose bush look passable. Inspiration just hadn't been striking like it used to. So, I'd been staring out the shop window again, watching happy people enjoying the sun, like I was some morose garden ornament until a voice startled me.

"Hey, I think we need to talk."

It was Britt, my shop manager and best friend. Those words never prefaced anything good.

"What about?" I asked carefully.

"I think you need to take a step back." Britt fixed on the scuffed wooden floor.

"Well, yeah, before I behead this entire rose bush I should probably get some water." I tried to make a joke, but the knot of confusion tightened in my chest.

"Lea, you've been working yourself to the bone since… well, since everything happened." Her voice faltered, and

I understood she was trying to be sensitive. She didn't want to say, "since your mom died" out loud.

"Ah." I didn't comment further, pressing my lips together as I returned to carefully snipping at the wilting petals of the truly hopeless rose bush perched by the window. The room fell into silence, Britt watching me closely while I avoided her eyes, focusing on the gentle rustle of leaves and the soft thud of petals hitting the floor.

"Ah? Ah... what?" she finally asked. "Ah as in 'Ah, Britt is right and the wisest best friend in the world' or 'Ah, I'm going to pretend I'm listening but won't do anything about it'?"

I pursed my lips and rolled my eyes. She was right. Deep down, I knew it, and she did too. But I wasn't ready to give in just yet.

"Ah, Britt is right, but maybe I'm not ready to admit it?" I said after a long, deep breath, my voice tinged with reluctance.

"I thought so." She gently, but efficiently, took the shears from my hands and guided me to one of the worn chairs nestled behind the cash register. She squeezed in beside me, our knees touching like we were just two teens swapping the day's gossip again, and not two adults coping with one of the worst things that could possibly happen.

We sat without speaking, listening to water drip through planters and the cooler for the cut florals click on in the background. Britt was waiting for something, I could tell. Everyone wanted progress reports on my grief, like it was something I could move through and check off my list. Lea, done with mourning, situation normal.

No one wanted to hear that it didn't work that way.

"Well?"

"Well." I scrunched up my face, trying to hold back tears and failing. "Well. I just can't be here without thinking about her. I see her everywhere. It's like her ghost is following me around." The words hung in the air.

Britt grabbed my hands as she watched the tears stream down my face. "Then you need to stop. You need a fresh start, away from the old memories."

"What do you mean?" I bristled, already on the defensive.

I didn't want to close the shop. It hurt right now, sure, but my mom had been so proud of it. I couldn't give that up just because I was feeling sad. Mom wouldn't want that for me.

"The shop is doing great. I know you have been able to put away a big chunk into savings and that your mom's life insurance policy has you set for more than a few years. What if you opened a second location?"

I blinked. That isn't at all what I'd expected her to suggest. My mind started running with it immediately. I did have the cash to open a second location, I could even pay the deposit in up front. Mom had ensured I wasn't left in need. A second location to put my own stamp on? To start all on my own? I suddenly felt excited for the first time in months.

I grabbed Britt in an impulsive hug. She only froze for a second before squeezing me back. It took a little while to collect myself, but as soon as the tears slowed, my brain started whirring through lease agreements and possible locations. Somewhere that didn't have my mother's handwriting on every sticky note, her perfume lingering in the storeroom—just a blank slate.

"I can't believe I didn't think of this," I said, dashing the back of my hand across my face. "I thought you were going to make me do yoga or see a therapist."

"I still think you need a therapist," she said, leaning forward so her elbows rested on the counter, "but at least this is more fun than downward dog."

I laughed, choked and snotty, but it felt good. It made the weight in my chest a little lighter. "I'm going to do it," I said. "I'm going to open my own shop." The final syllable hung in the quiet, dusty sunlight like a promise.

Now I stood outside of the building I'd purchased, sight unseen, with my hands on my hips and head cocked to the side, taking it all in. The real estate agent wasn't lying. It was in dire need of some love. The paint was chipped and faded and the wood underneath looked worn and possibly as if it had some water damage.

I was here in Hallow's Cove on somewhat of a stealth mission. I'd booked a room at the inn and told the lovely rabbit shifter owner and receptionist, Judy, that I was just visiting and needed a quiet weekend away. What I really wanted was a chance to get to know Hallow's Cove and some of its inhabitants without a giant "New Girl" sign painted on my back. Another reason I was up with the sun, surveying my purchase before the rest of the town woke up. I'd already looked through the inside in the

4

barely there morning light. It had been a clothing shop before so it needed some work before it could become a flower shop, but nothing crazy. Even better it had an adorable two-bedroom apartment above it. It was bare and dusty—and in need of furniture—but it was mine.

I stopped wistfully thinking about different colors of trim and what plants I would proudly display in the gorgeous (and somehow still intact) original windows, when my stomach grumbled. Judy told me that Ted's diner opened early so I headed over, thinking about scrambled eggs and hash browns. Luckily, it was only one shop down from mine, past the bookstore, which looked charming, but was oddly just named "Bookstore."

That got my wheels turning as to what I wanted to name my new shop. I was completely lost in my thoughts when I opened the door to Ted's and ran directly into a brick wall.

I stumbled back half a step, blinking rapidly. My heart thudded in my chest, adrenaline singing in my veins—because I had barreled straight into a wall of muscle. A wall that huffed softly through flared nostrils.

I tilted my head back. And then kept tilting it. Up and up until my eyes met a pair of rich amber ones, flecked with gold. The minotaur towering over me quirked a single brow, clearly amused by the frazzled human who'd just ricocheted off his chest like a moth slamming into a window.

I'd come to Hallow's Cove fully aware that monsters made their homes here. It was kind of why I chose it. I wanted to get away from the city and set my sights on new experiences. Still, up until now, I'd only met the rabbit shifter family that ran the inn.

This, however... this man was no rabbit shifter.

He was massive. Broad-chested, thick-armed, and every inch of him exuded quiet, tethered power. His horns curved back in elegant arcs, polished and gleaming white, and one of them had a shallow nick in the side. I couldn't stop staring, couldn't even remember how to close my mouth. A ridiculous thought flitted through my mind: There's no way he fits in a diner booth.

That's when I realized I was still in his way—mouth open, rooted to the spot like a human-shaped traffic cone.

"New in town?" he rumbled, his voice so low it vibrated through the soles of my shoes.

I nodded mutely, and his gaze roamed over me, not in a leering way but in the curious, assessing manner of someone used to seeing who came and went through a small town. His lips tugged into a slow grin, equal parts warm and wicked.

"Sorry about that," I mumbled, stepping aside and feeling heat bloom in my cheeks. "I wasn't paying attention."

The grin deepened, and suddenly his whole face changed. The initial stern lines softened, replaced by something that felt disarmingly genuine. That smile made him seem less like a legendary beast and more like a man who might hold doors open and laugh at dad jokes.

"Not a problem." He gave a casual shrug, then gestured toward the exit. "Maybe I'll see you at Killy's bar tonight.

They've got live music on the weekends." He paused. Then winked. A slow, deliberate thing that made my stomach flip like a pancake.

And then he left.

I stood there for a beat too long, trying to reboot my brain. A minotaur just winked at me. A handsome, giant minotaur just invited me to a bar. I'd come to Hallow's Cove for a new start, fresh from the grief of losing my mom, but I hadn't put any thought into romantic pursuits. I suddenly started thinking of all the other places a minotaur wouldn't fit and found myself blushing to my roots. What would it be like to be held by someone that big?

A soft voice brought me back to the present. A faun waitress had appeared beside me, her hooves clicking gently on the linoleum floor. Her curls bounced as she tilted her head and gestured toward a booth in the corner. She didn't even bat an eye at my deer-in-headlights expression. Just led me to what had to be the most oversized booth in the place. I got the feeling I was just one in a long line of outsiders trying to adjust to the reality of monsters being in town living their everyday lives. And sometimes being ridiculously attractive.

The faun tapped her pen on the pad she held, bringing me back to the diner. I decided on a breakfast burrito and coffee. The faun returned with coffee and creamer.

"Ted doesn't mess with fancy espresso drinks." She nodded toward the Bigfoot manning the griddle "But if you are more of a latte gal, Cool Beans is the place to go for coffee in town." The town must be really tight-knit if she was willing to tell me that there were better places to get coffee.

Once she was gone, I pulled my notebook out of my bag and started jotting down first steps for renovating the space. My contractor in the city had recommended one here in Hallow's Cove and I was due to meet him back at the flower shop early that afternoon. I wanted to have a list of priorities in hand, but I got lost in thought and started doodling little flowers similar to the ones I anticipated painting all over the shop. I loved painting and had even gone to art school when Mom insisted I get a degree before taking over the flower business. She never wanted me to feel like taking over the shop was my duty.

Despite my passion, Mom couldn't grasp my desire to take over the flower shop. After spending a year immersed in art school, learning about color theory and design principles, I returned with a vision to revitalize the business. Mom's work was amazing, with lush arrangements and vibrant colors, but as was true with everything, trends were shifting and Mom wasn't keeping up anymore. People were looking for new and different ways to arrange flowers at events—more abstract and modern designs that broke away from traditional styles—and even just in a regular bouquet, they wanted something fresh.

Eager to infuse new life into the shop, I worked alongside Mom in my early twenties. This business had deep roots; my grandmother, Daisy, had started it during a time when women of color rarely owned businesses and passed it onto my mother, Dahlia. Now it was time for me, Azalea, to continue in their footsteps.

Things were going smoothly, with me learning the ropes and adding my creative flair, when Mom fell ill.

Designing the floral arrangements for her funeral was a heart-wrenching task I hadn't expected to face so soon. I carefully selected the finest dahlias to honor her memory and scattered her ashes among the wildflowers in the preserve near our home, a place she had always loved.

And now I was here, in Hallow's Cove, at Britt's urging, and I hoped beyond hope that this would be a new place for me to set down roots.

Back at the shop, I was waiting on a contractor that I had to assume would be a monster, but had no idea what type. I peered through the shop's window and saw a giant form approaching me. This had to be Randy. He was easily seven feet tall and that wasn't counting the dark gray horns that sprouted from his brow and curled backward.

He stepped through, lowering his head so his horns would fit. I tried to keep myself from gasping audibly as he entered the shop. If I thought the minotaur from the morning was huge, he had nothing on Randy. This guy had to be over seven feet of green-gray skin. I cocked my head to the side, trying to take him all in. He had to be an ogre. An ogre in his... fifties? His tusks were incredibly long, pointing upward past his broad nose. His long black hair was tied back with a leather strap and graying at the temples.

As the door closed behind him, he flicked his yellow eyes up and down me.

"You Lea?" he asked in a gravelly voice.

"That's me! Are you Randy?" I put my hand out to shake his, but he already had a clipboard and pencil out.

"Yep. I am. And you want to turn this into a flower shop?" He looked around the space, lips pursed. I wondered if he was thinking this new city girl was out of her depth.

"Well, flowers and plants," I hedged, nervous all of a sudden.

"Hmm," was all he responded as he started walking the space.

Was that a good *hmm* or a bad *hmm*? I followed him, trying to read the notes he was taking on his clipboard, but he was too tall. He meandered the shop for several minutes before finally turning to me.

"Is there anything you want in particular?"

"I would love to keep the original windows if that's possible. And I need more shelves. A lot more shelves."

He nodded and scribbled more notes down on his clipboard. His expression was unreadable—I had no way to tell if he found these requests reasonable or not.

"And what kind of flowers do you plan to sell?" he asked eventually.

"Oh, all sorts! I love being able to use locally grown flowers, but also have great relationships with wholesalers that work with hard-to find flowers and—"

He cut me off. "Do you think you'll carry tulips?"

Tulips had a season so they were only available part of the year, but they were a fairly standard flower to keep on hand.

"Yes, of course. Tulips and bulbs, in case anyone wants to plant their own."

The ogre's face broke into a big smile. "My wife loves tulips and has the worst luck getting them to grow. I am sure she will be happy to have you in town."

"I would love to help her plant tulips!" Maybe this was it. Maybe I really could fit in here. Something in my chest relaxed.

Maybe I could be happy again

"Well, let's get you settled here first and then I can drag you over to meet Beth." He went back to his notepad. "I can get you up and running in six weeks, maybe less. Does that work?"

I beamed at him. Good contractors were hard to find. A six-week timeline was a huge win. It would give me time to start ordering flowers and getting the word out that the town now had a florist.

"That sounds amazing!"

"Alright, I will get my team ready and we will start Monday morning."

I stuck out my hand to shake his in agreement and he didn't hesitate. "It is going to be a pleasure working with you, Ms. Thompson."

"Please, call me Lea."

"Alright, Lea. I'll see you Monday morning."

Chapter Two

Rick

I OPENED UP THE shop just after leaving Ted's. It was Sunday, so I didn't open until 10:00 a.m., giving me plenty of time for a leisurely breakfast. Most days, I made do with a protein shake—fast, efficient, forgettable. But on days I opened late, I treated myself. An omelet loaded with cheese and hot sauce, or maybe French toast if I felt like indulging. I liked my routines. They kept things predictable.

But this morning felt different.

As I rolled up the metal shutters at the front of the shop, my thoughts kept straying back to the tiny human I'd quite literally run into at Ted's. She was new in town, that much was obvious. I'd never seen her before, and I made it a point to know every face that passed through Hallow's Cove.

She'd looked up at me with those wide brown eyes, like she couldn't decide if she'd just collided with a man or a myth. Her skin was a rich, warm walnut, with an almost ethereal glow that seemed to radiate from within, casting a gentle light on her surroundings. Her riot of dark curly hair framed her face in a way that made her features stand out—soft, open, and utterly human in a way that felt rare around here. And those lips... full and lush, parted just slightly when she stared at me. It was innocent, uncalculated.

I wondered if she'd show up at Killy's tonight like I'd hinted. I wasn't usually that forward with strangers, especially humans. But something about her short-circuited my filter.

How long had it been since I'd been truly interested in someone?

Not since Angela, a harpy from a few towns over. That had fizzled out six months ago. She was nice enough, smart, funny in a dry way, but our needs never lined up. Literally. She had almost no sex drive, and while I respected that, it wasn't something I could ignore. A minotaur bull in his prime needed more. Denying that part of myself felt like going hungry in my own house.

We weren't a match, and we both knew it.

The break was clean, amicable. But since then? I hadn't met anyone who sparked my interest. Until this morning.

As I flipped the open sign and fired up the register, my thoughts drifted back to the curly-haired stranger. She didn't look like she belonged in a place like this, which made me wonder if she was trying to belong. That struck a chord in me. I had been there once. In Hallow's Cove, no less.

The bell over the door jingled and I shook myself out of my head. A young faun approached the counter, balancing a pile of mismatched hardware in her arms. That was the norm around here—ambitious DIYers who barely knew the difference between a screw and a nail.

"Hi," she said, tentative. "I'm trying to mount shelves in my house, but none of the screws are working. They just spin and spin and make a cloud of dust everywhere."

I forced on a smile, my tail flicking the only tell I was irritated. "Sounds like you've got lath-and-plaster walls. You'll need toggle bolts and anchors. Regular screws won't hold."

After a few minutes of back and forth, I got her sorted, but I had little faith she'd pull it off on her own. Odds were good Randy would end up fixing whatever she tried. The grumpy old ogre had a soft spot for anyone attempting to be self-sufficient. That's what I liked about Randy—he didn't make a show of it. He just helped.

I stayed busy through the rest of the day, a steady stream of customers flowing in and out, but my mind wasn't on drywall anchors or torque settings. It kept circling back to the woman in the diner. I found myself wondering what kind of books she liked. If she had a favorite drink. If she'd wear that same curious look on her face if I kissed her.

Would she even be interested in someone like me?

It was barely six when I locked up shop early. I told myself I needed a break, but the truth was, I needed a shower and a clean shirt. If there was even a chance she'd be at Killy's, I wanted to be ready.

I picked out my best button-down and a pair of dark jeans that hugged my thighs and made my ass look good. I threaded my tail through the back hole and buttoned up, giving myself a once-over in the mirror. My horns were polished, my hair combed back, and I'd even spritzed on the cologne I usually saved for dates.

I felt like a teenager before prom. Ridiculous.

But I hadn't felt this kind of anticipation in a long time. Not the raw lust—that was easy. This was something else. The kind of interest that made me wonder what her laugh sounded like in a quiet room.

I gave the mirror one last glance. I looked good. I just hoped she was into monsters. I had been on dates with humans before, but nothing serious. Who was I kidding? I rarely committed to anything serious.

The moment I stepped into Killy's, the comfort of the place wrapped around me like a worn leather jacket—familiar music, warm lighting, the scent of fried onions and spiced cider in the air. Brooks waved from the corner. Gwen and Gabe were already deep in a game of darts, and Jake and Hayley were talking animatedly over shared pints.

Harley, polishing a glass behind the bar, gave me a grin. "The usual?"

"Yeah. And start a tab," I said, sliding my card across the counter. "Might be here a while."

She poured my snakebite without a word. I took a slow sip, eyes already scanning the crowd—and found her.

The woman was here, standing near Randy and Beth, her curls pinned up in a charming halo. She wore a soft green dress that caught the light when she moved. Not flashy. Just effortlessly radiant. She was laughing—genuine and bright—and something twisted in my chest. Randy and Beth don't usually hang around newcomers. For them to stick close meant they liked her. Maybe she was more than a tourist passing through.

I forced myself to turn away, giving my attention to Gabe, a gargoyle, and Gwen, his human wife. They ran the town's game store, Gargoyle's Games. But Gwen noticed my distraction immediately.

"At it again?" she said, taking a sip of her gin and tonic. "Subtle, you are not."

"Huh?"

She jabbed a thumb toward the new girl. "That's the third time in ten seconds you've looked over there. Go."

I smirked, caught red-handed. "Alright, alright."

I crossed the floor slowly, wiping my hands on the back of my jeans. Must be condensation from the snakebite. My palms didn't normally sweat this bad

"Hi there," I said, stopping just behind her shoulder. "I seem to remember meeting you this morning."

She turned, startled at first, then smiling with recognition. "Oh. Right. Sorry again." She extended her hand. "Lea. Visiting for the weekend."

Ah, so she was a tourist.

I took her hand, warm and small in mine. "Rick."

She held my gaze a beat longer than polite, then looked away. "Sorry, I'm not usually this... flustered."

"I'm not usually this intrigued," I replied before I could stop myself.

We both blinked.

I cleared my throat. "So, what brings you to Hallow's Cove?"

"Needed to get away. The city's... a lot. Work, noise, people. I thought I'd come someplace quiet to breathe."

I nodded. "You picked the right spot. Cell coverage is terrible, and the Wi-Fi's a joke. Great for vanishing."

"Exactly what I wanted."

Beth and Randy drifted away somewhere mid-conversation, and we didn't even notice. The two of us sat down at a high-top, and she asked about the town, how I ended up here, what it was like to live among monsters.

"I didn't grow up here," I explained. "But my grandparents did. After my parents died, they raised me. Gave me everything, even when I didn't know how to ask for it. I guess I came back to Hallow's Cove because I wanted a quiet life. Something I could build on my own."

She looked at me differently then—not with pity or fascination, but with understanding. Like she knew what it meant to lose something and start over.

"That's really beautiful," she said softly. "I think that's kind of what I'm doing too. Starting over."

When her drink was nearly gone, I offered to get another. Her order caught me off guard.

"A snakebite?" I echoed, raising a brow.

She shrugged with a smile. "I dated a Brit in college. Picked up the habit."

I went to the bar, half-smiling to myself. A woman who drinks snakebites and doesn't blink at a seven-foot minotaur? Dangerous combination.

When I returned, she accepted the pint with a grateful nod, our fingers brushing for a second too long.

Lea's eyes floated over the crowd, then back to me. "So if you grew up somewhere else, what did little Rick want to be before he ran a hardware store?"

I snorted. "Little Rick wanted to be a professional wrestler. My grandpa had all these old tapes—guys in leotards and masks jumping off ropes. I'd practice suplexes on bags of mulch out back until I split them open. He'd make me sweep it up. Said if I was gonna make a mess, I'd better learn how to clean it." I shrugged. "Didn't pan out. Turns out I hate spandex."

Lea grinned, leaning in. "But you still get to lift heavy things all day and boss people around. Living the dream."

"Exactly. And the dress code's more forgiving."

She rolled the glass between her palms. "I always wanted to be an artist. My mom said I started drawing before I could walk. Family legend says I accidentally customized our living room walls with permanent marker at age three."

I couldn't help but laugh, picturing her as a curly-haired toddler, joyfully vandalizing her home. "Bet your mom was thrilled."

"Oh, she was delighted," Lea said, deadpan. "Said it added character. She framed a chunk of the wallpaper, actually. She was sentimental like that."

"Sounds like a good mom."

"She was." The words came out soft, wistful, and she glanced away, clutching her glass. "Sorry. I keep doing that thing where I talk about her like she's still around. She passed last year"

"I get it." Maybe I shouldn't have, but I reached across the table, covering her hand with mine. Her skin was warm, her pulse thumping steady beneath my thumb. "Sometimes I still talk about my parents in the present tense. Feels less weird than saying 'were' all the time."

Lea's lips curved, slow and grateful, like the compliment wasn't about her but about something she used to belong to. Her hand stayed where it was, under mine, and I realized I didn't want to pull away. In a room full of people, we'd managed to make our own quiet corner. I liked that.

She cleared her throat. "So, what do minotaurs do for fun in a place like this, other than wrestle and terrorize new girls at the diner?"

"Oh, the usual," I replied, straight-faced. "We stampede through the farmers market, devour hay bales, and challenge tourists to feats of strength. Sometimes, if we're feeling really wild, we reenact famous labyrinth scenes for the elementary school."

She snorted, nearly losing her beer. "I'd bet money you were in marching band, not football."

"Wrong on both counts," I said with a wink. "Debate club. National champion, two years running. I even went to State. Turns out, when you're the loudest kid in the room and half the judges are terrified of you, you rack up trophies quick."

Lea actually clapped, the sound ringing out above the low hum of the crowd. "I can see it. You've got a definite, like... 'Order in the court!' vibe."

"And you?" I asked. "Let me guess: theater kid."

She looked affronted. "Excuse me, I was a proud member of the—drum roll, please—poetry club."

I grinned. "So, you sat in cafés and judged everyone's metaphors?"

"Only the bad ones," she said with mock seriousness. "But we also hosted open mics. I once read a poem about a dying houseplant that made someone cry. At least that's what she claimed—it might have been my outfit."

I leaned in, elbows on the table, feeling that pull—the magnetic force that happened when two people landed in the right conversation at the right time, and neither was quite ready to let the moment go. Not only was she was funny and quick-witted, our shared loss made it easy to connect immediately.

We kept talking, falling into that easy rhythm people chase their whole lives and rarely find. She told me about losing her mom and learning to stay afloat without her.

As the bar thinned out, her hand grazed my arm again, casual but deliberate. Her fingers lingered. My skin buzzed.

"So," she said, tilting her head coyly, "do you have somewhere to be in the morning?"

"Nope," I said, holding her gaze. "Just me and my morning off."

She bit her lip, then let it go slowly. "Well, would you like to head back to the inn with me—for the night?"

Her voice danced with laughter, yet her eyes spoke of something more—something hungry, something hopeful. I didn't know where this night would lead, but I felt a fierce pull I didn't want to let slip.

"You're right. It's too early to end the night here," I murmured, my hand slipping over hers.

Chapter Three

Rick

We downed the last of our drinks and I settled the tab. Lea wound her arm through mine as we walked under the pale lamplights of Hallow's Cove's empty streets. Our conversation continued loose and free as we approached the inn and quickly entered the open elevator—as if it knew we were coming.

When the elevator doors closed, the air crackled between us. Lea slid her hands around my waist, drawing me into her warmth.

"Hi," she breathed in the close quarters.

"Hi, yourself," I responded cheekily.

Lea snaked her fingers up my arms and around my neck, pulling me in for a kiss. I'd kissed a human before, but I'd forgotten how much smaller their mouths were. At first I hesitated, knowing my much larger tongue could overwhelm her, but Lea had no such hesitation. It didn't take long for us to find a rhythm and Lea wasn't shy. She sucked on the tip of my tongue in a way that only meant one thing, and it wasn't long before I had her up against the wall of the elevator, pressing my hips into hers.

The machine pinged, alerting us that we were on Lea's floor, and I released her, painfully aware of the erection growing in my pants. She took my hand in hers, pulling me down the hall. She pulled out an old-fashioned room key and stopped at a room halfway down the hallway, taking a moment to unlock her door.

As soon as we were inside, I pinned her to the back of the door, caging her in with my arms as I devoured her with my lips. Her soft gasps and moans as I sucked and licked her mouth were magical. She was so responsive to my touch. I wrapped my hand around her neck and pulled her even closer, our bodies pressed against each other.

But with the height difference, it wasn't long before I wanted her even closer. I wrapped my arms around her waist and lifted her up against me, causing her to let out a surprised squeak mid-kiss. My thickening cock was now right up against the junction of her thighs. Whether conscious or not, she was already grinding against me.

Her dress bunched at my hips, and I felt her heat through her underwear. My pulse hammered through me, like speakers at a concert making each of my limbs resonate. I wanted to savor every inch of her, starting with her round cheeks all the way down to her toes.

I took her wrists, gently, and stretched her arms above her head. "Keep them there," I growled, not even bothering to mask the need in my voice.

She grinned wickedly. "Yes, sir."

I let her legs down slowly. She stayed pressed to the door, obedient, her hands braced just above her head. I stepped back, just enough to drink her in. She watched me through her lashes, pulse visibly ticking in her neck.

Her dress was stretchy and soft, the kind that clings and then bounces back into shape. I curled my palms around her waist, thumbs pressing into the slight indent above her hips. I let my gaze drag over her, taking in the goosebumps that rose on her skin where the green fabric left her arms bare. She shivered, her breathing shallow.

"Tell me if this is too fast," I said, voice rough.

She shook her head, insistent. "I want this."

God, she did. Her thighs trembled when I skimmed my hands down, pausing at the hem of her dress, then beneath it. Her skin was soft, so soft I wanted to bruise it with my teeth. I ran my hands up the backs of her legs, not stopping until I cradled her ass. She moaned, a small needy sound that nearly undid me.

Her lips found my jaw, then my neck, her tongue flicking against a pulse point that made me grunt and clutch at her hips. I rolled my cock against her through the barrier of pants and panties, and the friction made her gasp. She bit my neck—sharper than I expected—and then licked the spot, as if apologizing.

I'd never been with someone so unreserved, so fundamentally hungry for touch. Even the monsters I'd known tended toward self-restraint, as if we all believed that if we let our control slip, it'd end up ugly.

She pressed her chest against me like she wanted to fuse herself to my body. I obliged, greedy. My hands snaked to the neckline of her dress, the clingy fabric already straining with the rise and fall of her breathing. She was so responsive—every touch, every press of my lips, seemed to set her on fire.

"Can I?" I rumbled softly, fingers catching on the hem of her green dress.

"Yes," she whispered, her hands bracing still above her head, but her hips bucking as she ground herself against my thigh.

I tugged, slow and careful, drawing the neckline down until both breasts spilled free—no bra, just soft skin tipped with perfect brown nipples that peaked impossibly tight in the cool air. I had a brief, worshipful pause. The sight did something to me, primal and dizzying.

I bent to take her nipple in my mouth, nipping gently. She gasped just as I hoped she would—a sharp, needy sound that vibrated through her whole body. I switched to the other, teasing with my tongue before drawing circles with my thumb over what I'd just kissed. The scent of her—shampoo, sweat, that tart sweet tang of arousal—clouded my brain. I couldn't get enough of her.

Her hips rolled, desperate, seeking friction. I let my hand slide down her stomach, fingers grazing her underwear—already damp, already soaked through. I pressed my palm against her hot core and she moaned, loud enough that the sound bounced off the plaster walls. Grinning into her chest, I kissed down her feverishly hot skin from her neck to her collarbone to her stomach and then dropped to my knees.

Lea stared down at me, biting her lower lip in anticipation, hands still braced above her head like I'd told her. The sight sent a surge of anticipation through me. I hooked my thumbs under the waistband of her underwear and dragged them down, letting my knuckles graze her thighs as I went. She shivered again, but she kept her hands right where I'd left them.

I kissed up her bare legs, my tongue teasing the delicate crease behind her knee, then moving higher until I was level with her pussy. Oh, I was definitely going to have to be gentle with her. My mouth was eager, but I knew I had to take my time. Beneath her thatch of dark curly hair, she was wet and glistening, and her scent enveloped me—sweet, earthy, and absolutely intoxicating.

Her dark eyes burnt into mine as I lowered my head to her skin.

"God, you're beautiful," I murmured, letting my breath ghost across her skin.

She whimpered, her hips rocking forward in invitation.

"Tell me what you want," I prompted, my hands splayed across her thighs.

She inhaled shakily. "Please. I just—I want your mouth. I want to feel you."

I grinned, slow and predatory. "You want my tongue inside you, don't you?"

She pressed her back to the door, chest heaving. "Yes. Please, Rick."

Fuck, that did something to me. I parted her thighs gently, stroking the inside with my thumbs until she trembled. Then I licked her, slow and broad from bottom to top, and she made a sound—soft but so desperate I nearly lost it. Her taste was unreal, something sharp and sweet, like honey and salt and her.

I circled her clit with the flat of my tongue, then sucked it softly, feeling her whole body jerk. "You're already so wet for me," I growled, and watched her shudder at my voice.

"Yes," she gasped, arching forward. "Oh god, please—more."

I licked her again, deeper and more demanding, and her hands finally broke formation, tangling in my hair and tugging just hard enough to tell me exactly what she wanted. I worked her, slow at first—lazy strokes, savoring every twitch—but her hips thrust into my mouth, demanding more. So I gave her more. I flicked my tongue over her clit, lapping at her until she was shaking, half-sobbing into her palm while she clamped one hand over her mouth. The other she kept tangled in my hair, as if afraid I'd stop before she shattered completely. The sight of her losing control made my cock impossibly harder—I was the one doing this to her.

I teased her with a thick finger, slipping it into her molten heat as my tongue danced and caressed her sensitive clit. The intense pleasure of her warmth gripped me, urging me to delve deeper. As she writhed with desire, I added a second finger, curling them both to caress that certain spot within her. My rough tongue continued its assault, driving her to the brink.

She came hard, with my name on her lips, her whole body tensing then falling slack against the door. I felt her pulse beneath my tongue. I kept licking her, even as the sensitivity set in, sending aftershocks through her small frame.

When I finally stood, she blinked up at me, dazed and eyes glowing, her hands grabbing desperately at my shirt. She wanted me naked, and the need in her gaze was almost enough to make me lose control. Almost. But not quite. If I only had the one night with Lea, I wanted to make this last.

Her fingers fumbled at my buttons, but I caught her wrists, folding them gently in my hands. "Are you sure?" I whispered. "I'm—I might hurt you if I'm not careful." I wasn't sure how to say I am much larger than human dudes without sounding like a braggart.

A dismissive snort. "You won't. I want you to." Her mouth found my jaw, biting with purposeful intent. "Less talking, more undressing."

She was relentless in her pursuit, a spiral of urgency. I let her peel my shirt off, let her hands roam over the expanse of my chest, broad and dusted with chestnut fur. She stroked up and down my arms, admiring the bunch and pull of my muscles as I flexed under her touch. She mouthed at my collarbone, my shoulder.

"If you keep touching me like that, I'm going to lose control," I groaned, and she laughed—a bright sound that made my blood surge. I lowered my mouth to her neck, sucking her soft skin.

Lea arched up into me. Her hands found my belt next and within seconds she'd worked the buckle and button free, her fingers grazing the line of fur beneath my waistband. She hesitated only to look up at me, as if looking for permission, but her eyes were glassy and dark. Beyond the point of no return.

"Take me out," I whispered.

Her hand wrapped around my cock, and the shock of pleasure nearly doubled me over. I hissed between my teeth, bracing my forearm on the doorframe behind her head.

"Good lord," she said, the words tumbling out before she could catch them. Her hand had stilled, thumb tracing the swollen ridge at the head of my cock, and she looked up at me, eyes huge. "That's not even, like—that's not normal, right?"

I bit back a laugh and cupped her cheek, letting warmth fill my voice. "I can stop if it's too much. Really. I want you to feel good."

She shook her head, then blinked as if recalibrating. "No, I-I want to, I do, I just... wow." She gave a breathy laugh and wrapped her hand around me again, this time as if measuring, reassessing the territory. "I've never been intimidated by a dick before."

That made me bark out a real laugh, the tension shattering, and I kissed her forehead, her hairline, her jaw. "We can go slow," I said, voice guttural. "Or we can go hard. Whatever you want, Lea. You call it."

She didn't hesitate. She pressed herself to my chest, all softness and urgent heat, and whispered, "I want you to fuck me, Rick. I want to feel it tomorrow."

She said it like a dare. Like she already knew what I would do.

I braced her with a hand on her hip, aligning us. Even then, I took my time, letting the head of my cock trace slick circles through her folds. I watched her bite her lip, eyes fluttering, the muscles in her thighs trembling as she fought for patience.

"You're so big," she whispered, a mix of awe and hunger tinging her voice. "You're not going to break me, are you?"

I gave her a half-smile. "I'd never break you. But I might ruin you for anyone else."

I paused. We'd gotten so caught up I hadn't even thought about protection. It had been quite a while since I'd been so wrapped up in a partner I'd forgotten about protection. I froze, caught between the heady fog of need and the stinging sobriety of responsibility. I looked down at her, searching her face for any sign of uncertainty. There was none.

She must have read my mind. "I'm on the pill," she whispered, her thumb tracing the line of my jaw. "And I got tested after my last partner." She blinked, hopeful. "I'm good. Are you?"

I exhaled, the knot in my chest loosening. "Yeah. I get checked every few months. Just... wanted to make sure you were comfortable."

She nodded, and with a little laugh that was half relief, half anticipation, she hooked her heel behind my thigh and pulled me tight.

I lined myself up, careful, holding back—her body was so much smaller than mine, and I didn't want to hurt her, not even by accident.

"Ready?" I asked, voice half a growl, half a prayer.

She nodded, eyes shining with want.

I pressed in slowly, inch by impossibly sweet inch. Her gasp, sharp and unguarded, nearly undid me. She was so tight, her body stretching to accommodate mine, every muscle straining to take more. I rocked back, then deeper, easing myself in up to the ring halfway up my cock, pausing there. She was so small. I needed to go slow. But Lea surprised me. Notching her heel on my ass, right below my tail, she pushed me into her welcoming heat. Deeper and deeper, until I was buried to the hilt. For a dizzy, unreal moment, I stayed like that. The world could have ended. I wouldn't have noticed.

She moved first. Hips rolling up, greedy for friction, for fullness. I found a rhythm—deep and slow, not wanting to rush, just wanting to feel her. I braced myself on either side of her head, savoring the way she arched up, every writhe a small, electric shock that ran from my cock straight through my spine.

She clung to me, nails raking my arms gentle at first, then harder, until she left half-moon indents in my skin. I liked that, the proof she was losing herself. I wanted to hear her lose it, too.

"God, you're perfect," I breathed against her neck, biting her earlobe with my flat teeth. "You feel so fucking good, Lea."

She whimpered, head rocking back against the pillows, curls fanned everywhere. "More," she begged. "I want all of you."

"You really want it?" I pulled out just enough, slow and teasing, then thrust in again, a little rougher. "You want me to ruin you?"

"Yes," she gasped, "Please. Harder—"

I grabbed her ass, holding her in place, and upped the pace. The sound of us filled the room, skin slapping skin, her panting and my ragged grunts. I watched her face, every flicker of sensation, every gasp. She was getting close. Her whole body tensed, her pupils blown so wide the iris was just a sliver of color. My cock throbbed inside her, every squeeze and flutter making me want to lose control. But I knew I could make her come for a second time first.

"God, look at you," I growled, voice thick. "Taking every inch, so fucking brave. You like being split open, don't you?"

If she'd been shy, it was gone now; she clawed at my back, moaning into my shoulder. "Yes, yes, don't stop, don't—"

"I won't. You're doing so good for me. Fuck, you're perfect, sweetheart," I told her, hips slamming into hers with animal urgency. She locked her ankles at the small of my back, pulling me impossibly deeper.

I gripped her thighs, spreading them wider, and angled my hips until I could feel the flat head of my cock hit that spot that would make her go wild. She cried out, her body arching so sharply her shoulders left the bed. She was clinging to me like I might disappear if she let go. Her orgasm hit her hard—her whole body spasmed so suddenly I nearly came with her.

I slowed just a little, wanting to feel every shudder, to drag out the sweetness as long as she let me. When her spasms softened, I kissed her, gentle and grateful.

Only when she'd collapsed, boneless and glowing, did I let myself go. I pulled out, just enough for her to feel the stretch again, then slammed into her once, twice, three times, and came so hard it turned the world white around the edges. I emptied myself deep inside her, a roaring throb that left me shaking.

I fell into her, my full weight braced on my elbows, afraid of smothering her. But she only laughed, a breathless, delighted thing, and ran her hands up my arms, soothing every muscle like she'd known how much I'd worry.

We lay that way for a while, tangled and sticky and perfectly, silently attuned. Her head fit just under my chin, breath winding back to something even and slow. My own lungs steadied, my heart pounding with animal satisfaction of a male who'd found exactly what he didn't know he'd been missing.

I could have stayed like that for hours, but eventually Lea stirred, shifting her hips and letting me slip out. There was a low, decadent wetness between her thighs, and some of it smeared against my own skin. I grinned, unable to help myself. She caught the look and poked my side.

"Don't look so smug," she teased, though her lips didn't quite manage a straight line. "You're the one who almost broke the hotel door."

"I'll fix it," I promised.

Chapter Four

Lea

I WASN'T SURE HOW long we lay tangled up in the hotel sheets, but I was very sure that I'd never had sex like that in my life. Maybe it was the new place. Maybe it was the way Rick's body felt over and through and around me—massive, careful, and solid in a way that made me feel precious instead of breakable. Or maybe it was the simple, extravagant fact of being seen—really seen—by someone for the first time in what felt like forever.

His arm was warm and heavy across my chest, palm splayed and thumb absently tracing circles over my right breast. I stared up at the cracked plaster overhead, feeling the slow drip of sweat cooling between my shoulder blades, and realized there was no way I'd sleep. Not with every nerve ending still on high alert and the taste of him still sharp behind my teeth.

"Are you awake?" I whispered, though it was clear he was. His breathing had leveled out but his hand never stopped moving, like he thought I'd vanish if he let go. He rumbled a wordless reply, then nuzzled his lips into the crook of my neck. His horns bumped the headboard lightly as he shifted, and the faintest smile played at the edge of his mouth.

"Still here," he said.

"Good. I wasn't sure if you went to sleep with your eyes open, or if that's a monster thing, or..." I trailed off, realizing I might be in over my head. We'd just had possibly the hottest sex of my life, and I was already babbling about sleep habits.

"It's not," he said. "But I do have great hearing. You, though... you hum when you're content. Like a cat with a song in its chest."

I snorted out a laugh, shoulders shaking. The last person to tell me I purred was my mom, when she would set aside her Sunday to do my braids for the next few weeks.

I let the memory settle, warm and bittersweet, then reached over to snag the hotel water bottle from the nightstand. Rick made a low, appreciative sound at the stretch of my body and traced the curve of my waist with a possessive squeeze. My thighs ached but in a good way, like after a tough but fulfilling work out. My heart didn't quite know what to do with itself.

I took a long, grateful gulp and offered him the bottle. His hand dwarfed it, but he drank, then wiped his mouth with the back of his hand, eyes never leaving me—as if he was memorizing every detail. Like I was the marvel here, and not the seven-foot minotaur lounging naked in my bed.

"So, Rick," I said, snuggling deeper into his side, "is this the part where you tell me a dark secret about yourself?"

He snorted, a real, belly-deep sound. "Depends. You want the condensed version, or the full tragic saga?"

"I want all the dirt." I grinned. "You go first. I'll trade you one for one."

He seemed to think about it, then rolled onto his side, propped up on an elbow. The movement made his muscles flex, horned silhouette cutting a shadow across the wall. He was quiet for a moment—like he was weighing how much to say, or maybe how much to risk. I recognized the look. It felt almost identical to the one I gave strangers when they asked about my family.

He started talking, voice gone soft beneath the monster's boom. "My parents died when I was a kid. Car crash outside the city. I was, hell, six? Maybe seven. I barely remember them, just flashes. My grandpa would always say I got my stubborn streak from my dad, which... yeah, that tracks." He managed a crooked smile. "My grandparents took me in. Didn't really have a choice—no one else in the family wanted the responsibility, no one wanted a rambunctious kid that had a penchant for knocking things over."

He watched his own hand, knuckles rippling as he flexed the bottle between two fingers. "Grandpa was an old-fashioned minotaur. He owned dozens of hardware shops where I grew up in upstate New York. He never talked about feelings, but every morning he'd make me lunch and put it in the same brown bag, with a dumb cartoon on the side. Even in high school." Rick's mouth twitched again.

I reached up, brushing one of the ridges of his horn where it merged with the dark stubble of his scalp. I meant it as a joke, or maybe a comfort, but the intimacy of the gesture startled us both. His eyes flicked to mine, and the emotion there made my throat tight.

"You're a good storyteller," I said, and I tried for a laugh, but it came out too gentle.

Rick shrugged, but something about the movement was less contained now. "My grandma died when I was sixteen. Grandpa held on until my second year of college. After that, it was just me." His hand found my hip, thumb moving in slow circles. "I floated around from place to place for a long time. Hallow's Cove is the first time I put down real roots. Opened my shop, started sponsoring the town softball team. Pretended it was enough."

"Only, sometimes it isn't," I finished for him, and the words hit like a punch straight through my chest. I think it startled him. "It's never enough." I let my fingers follow the line of his jaw, the thick corded muscle there so different from any man I'd ever touched. "Not when you've lost people. That emptiness just... echoes, no matter how full your life gets."

He made a sound, something raw and almost angry, but he didn't pull away. "Yeah. That's it." His eyes flashed, then softened, all the bravado momentarily stripped away. "I keep thinking if I just do enough, work enough, stay busy enough, it'll stop hurting."

I'd lived by the logic since Mom's diagnosis. Pack the days so tightly there's no room for grief. Don't slow down, don't sit still, don't let the dark in, but sometimes, even when you're lying naked in a strange bed with a stranger who suddenly doesn't feel strange at all, the dark catches up anyway. And instead of running from it, you just sit with it. Or, in this case, lie chest-to-chest with it, and let someone else see what's left behind.

I blew out a long breath, feeling the words bubbling up in my throat.

Was I really going to talk about this?

"My mom died last year," I said, and I could feel my own voice wobble a little, but I kept going. "Cancer. It was fast. They told us six months, but she barely made it three. I took care of her at the end and, uh... I don't regret that, but sometimes I wonder if I lost myself along the way."

Rick's grip tightened around my waist, just a little.

"She owned a flower shop. Well, her mom did. Then she took it over, and then I did, and..." I trailed off, waiting for that familiar awkwardness to slide in between us. But Rick just held my gaze, warm and unflinching. It made the rest pour out.

"I loved the work—genuinely. I think it made her happy to know I'd keep the shop alive. But after she was gone, it felt like every order, every bouquet, was just a reminder that she wasn't there to see it. I don't even remember most of last summer, just the muscle memory of making arrangements and smiling at customers like nothing had changed."

I twisted the sheet between my fingers. "My best friend, Britt, called me out. She said I was killing myself slowly, clinging to the shop like it was a lifeline, but really I was just stuck."

I almost told him then—about the building, how I'd signed the deed and bought the fixer-upper, and how I was hoping to find my new beginning here in Hallow's Cove. But what would the end goal be? He'd said *only one night.* It wouldn't be fair to suddenly expect more.

I blinked and realized I'd let the room fall silent for a minute too long. Rick's eyes were heavy with understanding. I braced for a platitude, or maybe an awkward "sorry for your loss," but instead his thumb swept across my cheek—gentle, reverent. And then, to my absolute shock, I saw it: a single tear, bright and unmistakable, carving a path through the dark stubble at the corner of his eye.

He looked away, quick, almost embarrassed, and swiped it with the heel of his hand. "Sorry," he muttered, voice thick. "It's just—" He paused, looking back at me, and this time there was no filter. "I know what that feels like. To want so bad to move on, but not knowing the right direction to aim your feet." His words landed with the heavy, practical finality of a shovel hitting dirt, and something in me loosened.

"Do you always get this deep after sex?" I asked, only half joking.

Only I realized too late that I'd said "after sex," like this was a recurring event, like I assumed it would happen again. My face flamed, but Rick only grinned—wide and toothy, like I'd given him a present he wasn't sure he deserved.

"Only if the company's good," he said. "And the post-coital cuddling is excellent."

He drew me closer, big arms wrapping around me until my whole body was eclipsed by his. I let out a sigh and found myself sinking into him, into the pillow, into the hush of the small hours of the night. For the first time in months, maybe longer, my mind didn't immediately leap to a checklist of anxieties as soon as the adrenaline faded. It just... rested.

We drifted like that, talking quietly. He told stories about the townspeople, the way the monster and human populations tangled together here. I learned that Killy's Bar had an underground karaoke night that only regulars got invited to, and that there was a lake at the edge of town you couldn't swim in after dark, because the nixies got handsy. "They're not mean," Rick said, "but they'll try to drown you for a prank if you look like an easy mark." It was clear, the longer he talked, that this place was not simply a town he'd settled in by chance. I wondered what this town would look like with the sun up, with new flowers blooming in the window of a shop I might one day run.

Maybe tomorrow I'd tell him the truth. That I was here for keeps. That I'd signed my name on the ancient deed of the old clothing store, the one currently covered in dust and spiderwebs and possibility.

But not tonight. Tonight, I wanted to savor the afterglow and the raw connection with someone for only a brief moment. I relished the way my body still hummed from his touch, the way his palm held me like I was the answer to a riddle he'd been working at for years.

I closed my eyes for a minute, just to see if sleep would come. I was so used to fighting for rest that the quiet, sated heaviness felt like a miracle. Rick's breathing settled into a deep, even cadence, and the sound of it—so close, so sure—lulled me toward dreams.

Chapter Five

Rick

THE SUN WAS HIGH in the sky when I finally awoke, and my first thought was *Shit—the shop!* But then I quickly remembered I didn't open until noon on Mondays and nuzzled further into Lea's curls, grasping her around the waist where we still lay together in bed. I let myself sink into that moment, the heat of her soft body entwined with mine, her presence so vibrant even in sleep. I was tired, exhausted even, yet I felt more alive than I had in a long time. This woman had a way of disarming me without even trying, digging past my defenses, and that terrified me. I spent so much time thinking about Lea and how perfectly she fit against me, how I could get used to this—more than used to it. A life like this, with someone like her.

My stomach clenched at the thought of her leaving. The visit to the inn was supposed to be a one-time thing, a brief encounter that I wouldn't think about again. I was fooling myself if I thought I wasn't getting attached, her soft breaths puffing against my neck making that clear to me. I slowly extricated myself, careful not to wake her. She had me reeling, and I couldn't let that happen. It would mean nothing but heartache if I got attached and then she left.

I headed to the bathroom and splashed my face with cold water, letting the droplets run down my furred face as I stared into the mirror, trying to make sense of what had just happened. I looked away from my reflection and down at my junk. "That'll have to be taken care of," I muttered to myself as I grabbed a nearby washcloth. After cleaning up, I stood in the doorway for a moment, a strange flutter running through me as I took one last look at her in bed, still blissed-out from the night before.

I grabbed my pants from the floor and my shirt from where it hung on the back of the desk chair before I finally tore myself away, exiting quietly out of her room. I shut the door and headed back to my place to get ready for a Monday filled with shoppers who had no idea what they were doing.

It was early enough that I didn't pass anyone on the way to the shop, and I was able to shower. I was distracted by thoughts of Lea and it was barely more than three minutes to noon when I finally emerged from the shower, hastily putting on a T-shirt and jeans. I quickly rolled up the shutters, hoping it was early enough that no one from the inn would see me and recognize me as the guy who had left earlier that morning.

The afternoon passed in a blur of busywork and self-recrimination. I tried to focus on the shop, on the parade of customers who needed screen repair kits or rawhide mallets or window boxes they'd never actually install. I told myself it was for the best—better to keep things compartmentalized, to remember what happened last night and this morning for what they were: a bright, ferocious bloom that would wilt by Monday.

She said she was just visiting. She'd made it clear. And I wasn't about to get caught up in fairytales, no matter how good she looked straddling my hips or curled up against my chest.

Lea

The first thing I noticed when I woke was the ache—low and slow in my thighs, the memory of being expertly, extravagantly fucked. The second was the emptiness: the bed cold on his side, the sheets rumpled and smelling of minotaur and sex but not warmth. Not him.

He was gone. He'd left without saying anything. Not even a goodbye kiss.

I rolled over, pushed my face into the pillow, hoping to catch a phantom trace, but all I got was the chemical tang of hotel laundry beneath the smell of my own sweat.

I hated the sick swoop in my stomach, the little-girl longing for someone I'd known for less than twenty-four hours. I told myself it didn't matter. We had both said up front that this was a one-night thing. No promises, no strings. I could respect that. I'd even admired it, last night. Now, in the daylight, it felt like a door closing. Even if it was my own damn hand on the knob.

Still, it stung. I hadn't lied when I called myself a romantic—I'd just learned to keep those tendencies folded away, pressed and hidden under the weight of disappointment and practicality. But this? This was different. With Rick, for the first time in years, I'd felt something flicker to life.

Instead, I was alone. No note. Not even the hollow comfort of a "this was fun" scrawled on hotel stationery. Just emptiness and the undeniable sense that I'd been a fool to hope for more. I'd had a few one-night stands, but at least we exchanged numbers even if neither of us never called back. And if I was honest, none of them were like this.

I hauled myself upright, every muscle stretching and singing the memory of him. I stared out the window at the blank-sky morning, the sound of birds chirping and distant truck engines just sharp enough to remind me that this wasn't a dream. My hips ached pleasantly from the way he'd gripped me, the impact of our bodies echoing in every inch of skin. I was angry at myself for hoping. I was the one who had said this was only for the weekend—but there's no way that was normal for a one-night stand. Now I'm pissed at both of us for making it so much more than that.

Maybe it was the intensity of the whole thing—the fucking, the talking, the falling asleep tangled together, so close I could almost believe it was more than transactional pleasure. As I sat there, the anger bloomed and spread throughout me.

Had I been that bad? Was he just putting on a show, faking it the whole time? I'd thought we'd had chemistry, actual, honest-to-god chemistry, but now I wondered if I was just another notch in the bedpost—maybe not even a memorable one at that.

And that made me furious. I'd let him in all the way, shared things I'd never told anyone else—and all I got was a cold pillow and gnawing humiliation.

I balled up the sheets and threw them to the foot of the bed. Then I stared at the ceiling, the endless off-white expanse, and told myself to get it together. This was supposed to be a fresh start. If Rick wanted to ghost me, it was his damn loss. I was still me: stubborn, creative, maybe a little too sentimental. I could do this.

It got easier once I was upright and in motion. I tied my curls up into a poof using my satin headscarf, then showered, scrubbing my skin with unnecessary roughness, then dressed in my favorite overalls and a soft yellow T-shirt that made my complexion pop. I built the morning like a shield—protein bar, two cups of coffee, a full face of makeup even though I was only meeting Randy. But still, beneath the armor, I was sore. I was sad.

And I was definitely still thinking of him.

By the time I hit Main Street, the sun was high enough to bounce off every window and blind me with promise.

I pulled my bag tight across my body, told myself to walk like I was going somewhere worth being, and let the blooms lining the sidewalk remind me that things could always start over.

I rounded the corner to my new shop, the keys cold in my palm, and immediately froze in the middle of the sidewalk. The world had decided to take a direct, unfiltered piss on me. There, in the morning glare, the hardware store next door to my flower shop stood like a lighthouse of regret, its massive sign blaring HARDWARE.

But it didn't just say HARDWARE, as I'd noted the day before. It said Rick's HARDWARE, with the "Rick" in tiny cursive.

How had I missed that?

My face was hot, pulse pounding in my ears. My brain did a slow, reluctant pirouette. It was almost too on the nose—a cosmic prank so obvious I wanted to check the sky for hidden cameras. I felt the world tilt and I had to clutch my bag tighter, as if the weight of my embarrassment would otherwise tip me over. My mind jumped through every moment of last night, all the things I'd whispered in bed with a man whose shop—whose fucking name—was now staring me down at eye level.

Maybe it was a coincidence. But somehow, I knew it wasn't. I could feel it in the pit of my stomach, roiling, a slow chemical reaction that started as embarrassment and bubbled rapidly into something else.

Rage.

I stood there, staring up at the sign like the answer to my whole stupid life was just a matter of reading it correctly.

Rick's Hardware.

I marched straight to the door, the bell above it tinkling with the bright cheerfulness of someone who had never been abandoned in a hotel bed. The scent of sawdust and fertilizer hit me, acrid and grounding, but also layered with the faintest trace of the man himself—minotaur musk and whatever clean, citrusy soap he used. I followed the scent to the back of the store, where Rick stood behind the counter, forearms deep in a cardboard box of brass screws. He looked up, and for a split second his face did something—a ripple of surprise, or maybe regret. But then he schooled it, that practiced calm I'd found so stupidly irresistible the night before.

I didn't give him a chance to say anything. "Hey, neighbor," I snapped, my smile bright enough to cut glass. "Fancy running into you here. Or, you know, not running into you, since I thought you'd at least be polite enough to say goodbye."

He blinked, like he'd walked directly into a pane of glass. "Lea. I—"

"Save it," I said, slamming my palm on the counter. My vision was so tunneled on his face I barely registered the customer two aisles over, pretending to compare brands of duct tape while their eyes flicked over to us every ten seconds. "You know, I thought maybe you were busy. Or shy. Or that I'd read the night wrong. But you didn't even bother with the classic 'it's not you, it's me.'"

He squared his shoulders, but his hands gripped the counter like he was trying to hold the earth steady. "I thought you were just visiting," he said, voice even, but with an edge that wasn't there last night. "You said it yourself. One night."

My brain buzzed, a rising static that made it hard to hear anything except my own heartbeat. "So it meant nothing to you? You have nights like that all the time?" I tried to rein it in, but the words kept tumbling out, sharp and brittle. "At least give me enough respect to dump me to my face."

He was quiet for a minute, jaw working beneath the stubble. "It was a night. It was great. But that's what it was, Lea. You said—"

"I lied!" It came out so hard it startled even me. The word ricocheted off every angle of the shop, and the customer in aisle two abandoned all pretense and openly gawked. I steadied myself on the edge of the counter. "Yeah, I said that, but after last night, I thought maybe..."

And then it was too much, the tightness in my throat threatening to wring the words out as tears.

Rick stared at me, nostrils flaring in that slightly inhuman way, and for a second I thought he was angry. Then I saw it—the way his hands trembled, the way his jaw clenched like he was the one being flayed alive. "Lea, I—fuck. I thought you were leaving! I thought I was doing the right thing. I figured if I ripped the bandage off in the morning, it'd hurt less."

The rational move would be to walk away. To tell him thanks for the honesty, and then mind my own business, like everyone in my life had always done. But I'd never been rational, and yesterday had only proved it.

"I have to meet Randy in five minutes," I said, the words tumbling out before I could stop them. "We're starting demo over at the new shop."

Rick's brow furrowed. "You're opening a shop here?"

"Yeah. Next door." I jerked my thumb toward the street. "Grand opening in six weeks."

He blinked so slow I thought he'd malfunctioned. "You bought the old boutique?"

I almost laughed. "Guess you're stuck with me for at least the six months it'll take to realize I've made the biggest mistake of my life."

I turned on my heel and stalked out, the bell over the door jangling after me as I slammed it shut.

Chapter Six

Lea

THE SUNLIGHT OUTSIDE WAS too bright, the air too sharp. I barely made it to the curb before the tears came. Not a full breakdown—just a trickle, an overflow, a hot flush that threatened to drag my dignity through the gutter. I pressed the heels of my hands hard against my eyes, refusing to let anyone in this picture-perfect, happy little town see me cry. Not on my first official business day, not after everything I'd already survived.

But when I opened my eyes, there was Randy, leaning against the hood of a battered white van labeled "Moorhouse Contracting & Repair." He held out a disposable coffee cup, steam rising off the lid, and when he caught my look, he didn't flinch. If anything, he softened.

"Rough morning?" he said.

"Brutal," I replied, managing a wobbly smile as I accepted the coffee. It was hot, black, and tasted faintly of burnt caramel.

"Want me to break his kneecaps?" Randy asked.

Despite myself, I laughed. "You think he'd even notice? Guy's built like a steamroller." The joke didn't quite land, but the humor steadied me. I wiped under my eyes with the back of my sleeve, careful not to smudge my makeup.

Randy shrugged, mouth hitching up. "Maybe not, but I'm persistent. Besides, Beth always says it's the thought that counts." He regarded me sidelong, like he was measuring how much I'd let him see. "C'mon, let's go brutalize some drywall. It's good for the soul."

I followed him into the shop, the warmth of the coffee burning slow and steady down my throat. The building that would become my shop—mine!—looked marginally less derelict in the daylight. The windows glared with sun, the floors were sticky with time, and the corners were home to a city's worth of cobwebs. But it was mine, every splinter and stubborn floorboard.

We attacked the layer of old carpet and linoleum that covered the front half of the shop. Randy handed me a crowbar and a pair of battered gloves, and together we pried and peeled and hammered our way through decades of bad choices. By the time the rest of his crew arrived, the air inside was heavy with dust and the sound of our laughter banging off the high ceilings.

The crew was an eclectic mix—a banshee with a penchant for power tools, a hulking troll who worked with the care and delicacy of a jeweler, a pair of brownies who moved so quickly that I could never tell if there were two of them or just one in constant motion. I'd worried, in some distant, city-bred corner of myself, that I'd never fit in here—that the small-town monster vibe would swallow me whole. But within an hour, the entire crew had adopted me, folding me into their easy banter and letting me take the lead on every design decision, however small or ridiculous. It didn't matter if I was human, or a girl, or wearing mascara that probably made me look like a raccoon. They just wanted to build something good, and, for reasons I couldn't quite grasp, they wanted to build it with me.

By late afternoon, we'd unearthed the original hardwood floors, battered but beautiful, and I was up to my elbows in wood putty when Randy called a halt. "Let's pack it in for the day," he bellowed, clapping his hands so loud dust snowed from the rafters. The crew dissolved in a flurry of goodbyes and see-you-tomorrows, and in two blinks the shop was empty except for me and Randy, who surveyed my progress with a critical but not unfriendly eye.

"You did good, kid," he said. "Most folks would've tapped out after an hour of demo."

I wiped sweat off my brow, grinning in spite of myself. "My mother would rise from the grave if I abandoned a project halfway."

Randy laughed, a big, rattling sound that seemed to vibrate the whole shopfront. "Remind me never to underestimate you with a parent like that." He squinted, sizing up the bones of the place, then looked back at me with a kind of pride I hadn't seen since Mom's last good day. "This'll shine up real nice. Once it's done." He hesitated, then placed a careful, paint-stained hand on my shoulder. "And hey—if you ever need to talk off the record, about anything, Beth's a world-class listener. She'll bake scones and not ask a single question until you've had at least two."

I felt a lump forming in my chest, but I only nodded, blinking hard against the grit in my eyes. "Thanks, Randy. For everything."

He snorted. "If you want to thank me, buy Beth a coffee at Cool Beans and agree to let her make you a pie for the grand opening. She's been looking for an excuse to try out her new brown butter crust."

I laughed, the exhaustion hitting all at once. "Deal. On both counts."

He nodded, then let his hand fall away. For a moment, we stood in companionable silence, drinking in the dusty, sunlit emptiness of the shop. It felt good—better than I'd ever have guessed. Like seeing buds on a young plant glistening with dew, right before the bloom.

When Randy left, I stayed back for a little while, savoring the quiet. I paced the length of the shop, imagining where the tables and displays would go, picturing sunlight falling in a thousand colors through vases lined up in the front window. I thought about what my mom would say—probably something about the importance of having fun even when everything was chaos. I remembered a time she'd flooded the counter with a hundred cheap keychains and insisted we arrange them in a rainbow, just to see if anyone noticed.

I missed her. I missed her so much. But for the first time in months, the missing wasn't just hollow—there was something alive growing in the space she'd left behind.

I left the shop in the early evening, the sky painted in improbable sunset colors: peach and blue, the clouds lit up from below like the world's best flower arrangement. My hands were raw, my hair full of sawdust, and my mood... not good, exactly, but better. I wanted to call Britt and tell her about the day, but part of me wanted to hold it close, keep it just for myself a little while longer. Like a secret I wasn't ready to share.

I puttered around the shop before heading to the apartment upstairs. In two days, I was supposed to have this place ready to sleep in. In two days, I'd be officially a resident of Hallow's Cove. The apartment was spacious for only one. I wandered around thinking about what furniture I could bring over from Mom's once I was more settled. I had the basics arriving in the morning: bed, fridge, tiny kitchen table. There had to be a grocery store in town that I could check out—so I had staples when the time came.

I locked the door behind me, set out down Main, and promptly realized I had no idea where the hell to find a grocery store. There were a number of shops I could have stopped at—Cool Beans was open late, and the faun barista had already tried to set me up with a punch card and a social life. But I wasn't in the mood for small talk. I took my coffee to-go instead, letting my feet lead the way, weaving through side streets and alleys until the houses began to thin and the air took on a different smell—cool, mossy, alive.

The park was on the edge of town, a long stretch of lawn bracketed by overgrown thickets and a lazy creek. I didn't mean to end up there, but as soon as I saw the sign—HAWTHORNE PARK, in peeling blue paint—I made a beeline for the bench nearest the water and sat, shoving my hands deep in my pockets. The sun was dropping fast and the trees threw long, dramatic shadows over the grass. The creek made steady music, nothing like the chatter and grind of the city. Here, the quiet was deep and stubborn, and it left too much room for my thoughts.

I sat there for a while, breathing in the bright, green scent of evening, and let myself unravel. I tried to replay the morning with Rick like it was a funny story, something I'd tell Britt and she'd roll her eyes at my taste in men, but the humor kept fading away before it took purchase. All I could do was stare at the water and think about how easy it had been last night to let him in. How he'd felt like a home I didn't realize I'd been missing. How I'd let myself hope, in the small, unguarded hours, that maybe, just this once, something good might last.

I'd spent my whole life pretending to be unbreakable, but it turned out that the only thing harder than being left was letting yourself be soft in the first place. How my mother had done that—year after year, heartbreak after heartbreak—was a mystery. I didn't have her patience or her faith. But sitting here, I realized I wanted to. Even if it meant looking like a fool sometimes.

A crisp wind picked up off the water, and I hunched my shoulders, pulling my knees to my chest. I tried to blink the tears away, but they kept coming—slow, embarrassing, but also weirdly relieving. I cried because somewhere in the marrow of myself, I already missed Rick, and I hated how easily that happened. I let myself cry until the sky went dark. I didn't even hear anyone approach when a woman about my age appeared in front of me. She had curly red hair and large hazel eyes.

"Are you okay?" she asked, brows raised.

I sniffed, embarrassed to be caught crying in public. "I'm fine."

Her eyes widened. "Are you sure?"

"Yeah, I'm—" I broke off, then tried to smile. "I moved to town and nobody told me the pollen count in Hallow's Cove was, uh, catastrophic." I wiped my face on my shoulder, trying to play it cool.

The woman laughed, the laugh of someone who has definitely lied about allergies before. "Oh, that's nothing. Wait until the sap spirits bloom. Last year, I cried for a week." She plopped down at the far end of the bench, hands tucked between her knees. "I'm Maisie."

The strange woman pulled a packet of tissues from her sweater pocket and handed it to me wordlessly. I wiped my eyes and blew my nose in a very unladylike fashion and took a big breath. The crying spell was done. I was still upset, but I was no longer on the verge of tears.

"Do you want to talk about it?" the woman asked.

I puffed out a breath of air, not sure what I wanted. But I knew I wasn't ready to go grocery shopping or worse, head back to my new place and risk running into Rick again. Even his name made him sound like an ass. I should have known.

I tried to shrug it off. "Just guy trouble. Or monster trouble, I guess." The words sounded ridiculous as soon as I said them, but Maisie just nodded.

"Don't worry, it's a town specialty." She bumped my shoulder lightly with hers. "We've all had our tour of Hallow's Cove heartbreak."

I tried to laugh, but it caught in my throat. I pressed the tissue to my nose, wondering how much of my makeup was left after the crying jag.

Maisie's mouth twitched in a smile she tried to hide. "So whose ass do I need to kick?"

I weighed the odds of opening up to a complete stranger versus pretending I was just fine and risking spontaneous combustion. In the end, my brain was too fried and my heart too stomped-on to keep playing it cool.

"It was a minotaur," I muttered, staring at my shoes. "Seven feet tall, devastatingly hot, and emotionally stunted. We had a night. It was... I thought it was something. But then he just—" I snapped my fingers. "Poof. Gone before breakfast. Acted like nothing happened. Now I get to spend all week pretending I'm only here to gut a derelict storefront, not because he made me feel something for the first time in forever."

Maisie let out a low whistle. "Ooof. Yeah, that tracks. There's always at least one minotaur who thinks he's being noble by ghosting a girl. Like they're sparing us instead of just making it worse." She grinned, but the kindness behind it took the sting out. "You'd think the horns would mean they know how to handle delicate things, but no. Always charging ahead, then surprised when things get messy."

I snorted, half laugh, half sob. "He said it was just one night. But it didn't feel like that." My voice went small. "It felt like more."

Maisie nodded, eyes soft and oddly ancient. "It always does, with the good ones. Doesn't mean you're crazy, just means you're alive." She stared out over the creek, legs swinging under the bench, like she'd done this before. "You know, you can always throw a rock through his window. No one would blame you."

I smiled, a real one, the first since the morning. "Maybe if I get bored this week." I brushed my hair out of my face. "I was actually on my way to find the local grocery store, before I decided to ugly cry in the park."

Maisie hopped off the bench and offered me her hand like she's just had an epiphany. "Come on. I'll show you. If you're going to stick it out in Hallow's, you need food, and probably a decent bottle of wine. Also, the produce section is a prime spot for low-stakes people-watching. I'll teach you the ropes."

I hesitated, some tiny, stubborn part of me wanting to wallow a little longer. But the larger part—the part that remembered what it felt like to be cared for, even in small, unexpected ways—took her hand.

The walk to the market was short; Maisie kept up a commentary on the houses we passed: that one's haunted, that one has a secret basement, the blue one with the porch swing is owned by a banshee who bakes cookies for every single funeral in town. I let her talk fill the empty places in my head, and by the time we passed the bakery and ducked into the small, bright market, I was almost convinced I could do this whole "new life" thing after all.

Maisie steered me straight to the produce aisle, somehow knowing exactly where the best fruit was hidden. She inspected a head of lettuce with the gravity of a surgeon, then turned to me with a sharp look.

"You want to know the secret to surviving here?" she said, voice low. "Don't let anyone convince you that what you're feeling is too much. This town is built on people who felt too much and did something about it."

She piled mushrooms and snow peas into a paper bag, her deft hands moving with rhythmic certainty.

"So what brought you here?" I asked, curiosity finally outweighing my self-pity. "You sound like you're a lifer."

Maisie paused, expression open, almost inviting me to see past the surface. "I moved here for a man. Or, technically, a vampire." She grinned, flashing slightly sharper canines than I'd noticed before. "Barnaby. He started the town over two hundred years ago. I met him when I came to town for a quiet break from my software job. We fell in love and eventually I convinced him to turn me."

I blinked at her, caught between awe and the slow, pleasant horror of realizing I might be talking to an actual vampire in the produce aisle. "Wait. Are you—?"

She rolled her eyes, good-natured. "Oh, don't get all weird. Most of what you think you know isn't true. I don't eat people. Or food for that matter, but Barnaby keeps a supply of cow's blood in the freezer. At first it was... honestly? Nasty. Like drinking a cold, rusty smoothie. But you get used to it. Survival mechanism, I guess."

She shrugged and tossed a bag of limes into my basket as if that explained everything. "There's always an adjustment period for new beginnings, right? You'll find your thing."

I eyed her, trying to see traces of the monster beneath the cardigan and jeans, but all I saw was a woman who might have also sat on a park bench and cried her heart out once, then made peace with it.

"Is it weird?" I asked. "I mean, do you ever... wish you could go back?"

Maisie considered. "Sometimes. Not often. There's stuff I miss, sure. The taste of real ice cream. A hot cappuccino. But mostly I like what I've got now." She bit her lip and leaned in as if sharing a truly illicit secret. "You know what the best part is about dying and coming back different?" She didn't wait for my answer. "You do everything you always put off. No more waiting for the 'right time'—the right time is every goddamn moment."

Her words hardened in my chest like a diamond—tiny, perfect, irreducible. The ache of the morning was still there, but it was edged now with possibility, something sharp and sweet.

Maisie marched us through the aisles, loading my basket with the skill of a seasoned operator. Sourdough, olives, dark chocolate.

"Trust me," she said, "chocolate is the only cure for heartbreak. Well, the only one that doesn't leave a permanent record."

I wanted to point out that heartbreak wasn't supposed to be fixed with food, but what did I know? My coping mechanisms so far had included avoidance, overwork, and the occasional ugly cry in public. Wine and carbs seemed like an upgrade.

"What about you?" Maisie asked as we waited in the checkout line, loading groceries onto the belt with brisk precision. "What are you gonna do now that your world's imploded?"

I thought about it. Really thought. The true answer was I had no idea, but sitting there with a stranger in the after-flare of a meltdown, I realized maybe that was sort of the point.

"I guess I'm going to open the shop," I said. "Make it beautiful, even if no one comes. Maybe forgive myself for needing a do-over. Learn all the monster gossip. Try not to fall for another emotionally illiterate man-beast."

Maisie beamed like I'd just passed a pop quiz. "That's the spirit, kid." She slid her card to the cashier, waving off my attempt to chip in. "You can pay me back later. I'm running a tab for all emotionally traumatized newcomers."

We left the market, arms full of heavy bags and something lighter, too—a sense that maybe the worst was behind me. Maisie walked me back to my apartment the long way, down streets I hadn't yet mapped. For a while, we didn't talk, just let the newness of dusk and the hush of the neighborhood fill the space between us. A row of handmade wind chimes caught the breeze, a careful hedgerow lined a well-lit street, and a single porchlight burned gold in the growing dark like a pole star.

I got the door open, and we navigated through the construction site that was the shop and headed upstairs. At that point, I really needed to let Maisie go. She'd helped me enough for one day.

"Okay, shoo." I waved my arms toward her after we deposited the last of the bags.

"What? No way. I have to help you put all the groceries away." She blew her hair out of her face, clearly sweating.

"No, really. You've done enough. And..." I hesitated. "Dare I say I've made my first real friend in Hallow's Cove?"

"Of course." Maisie pulled me into a tight hug, then let me go. "You're sure you don't want more help? Or just more company?"

"I'm sure. Go be with your vampire."

Maisie pulled me into another hug before heading out. Once she was gone, I sat down in the only chair I had so far—a single desk chair—and let myself relax for a bit. I was elated to have met Maisie but exhausted from the emotional trainwreck of a day. I let myself stare off into space for a bit before getting up to put away the groceries. I organized everything the best that I could with minimal furniture—the hand-me-down fridge from the former owner would work until mine arrived.

I looked at my watch. Somehow it was already 8:30 p.m. I needed to get back to the inn. I wasn't sleeping here yet because the rest of my things weren't due to arrive until Wednesday. I had learned most of the town in the two days I had been here, but I didn't really want to walk back to the inn alone at night. I quickly shoved the rest of the groceries in the fridge, before grabbing some candy to take back to my room with me and headed out.

I was lucky that Hallow's Cove only had a few main streets and I wasn't far from the inn. I waved at one of the many rabbit shifter children working the desk and took the stairs up to my room. Then I threw myself on the comfortable bed, utterly exhausted.

Chapter Seven

Rick

I SPENT THE HOURS after Lea left the shop in a kind of fugue—moving through the familiar motions, but with a persistent afterimage burned into my vision: her hands bracing the counter, her voice trembling with anger, the way she'd looked at me as if I'd yanked the ground out from under her and was now asking why she tripped. I bagged up orders, restocked the adhesive aisle, and repaired a couple leaky garden hoses, but all the while my mind stuttered around the simple, inescapable fact of her staying.

She hadn't been lying about the building; I'd watched through the front window as she and Randy's crew went after the old linoleum with a vengeance, crowbars gleaming in the light like swords in a war I'd already lost. She laughed at something Randy said and, even through the shared wall of our building, the sound hit me like a punch in the gut. I told myself I was keeping tabs to be a good neighbor. Maybe even to make sure she didn't fuck up the building's load-bearing beams.

That was a lie.

I watched because I wanted to know if she was okay. If she was still angry. If her face would go soft when the workday ended, or if I'd managed to break something I had no right to touch in the first place.

The worst part was knowing just how much of an ass I'd been. All the old self-protective habits had kicked in, like a fire drill for my heart, and I'd painted myself into a familiar corner: a well-fortified place, sure, but bleak, echoing, and just cold enough to remind me why no one stayed very long.

By sunset, the hardware store was quiet and I let myself drift through the aisles in a daze. I stood in the dark, empty store, and tried to remember the last time I'd felt this off-balance. Maybe never—maybe not since I was a kid, facing down a future with no parents and a list of questions that no one wanted to bother answering. That same feeling now—a bottomless, tilting vertigo—only this time, there was no distant grown-up promising it would get better. There was just me and a woman who had already wormed her way under my skin in less than a day.

I made a decision. I steeled myself. Be civil. Be indifferent. She lied, so she'd get exactly what she told me she wanted: a casual fling and a wave in passing.

Back in my apartment, above my shop, I disrobed into pajama shorts, trying to shake the perfect echo of her moans in my mind. I couldn't even distract myself with work projects, which usually drowned out anything emotional. The shop downstairs was silent, waiting for yet another new day to begin.

As I lay in bed, sleep eluded me. I kept tossing and turning, my thoughts churning. What if I ran into her tomorrow? I wanted to act chill, be normal. But that didn't seem possible. It was already past midnight, and still every second with her flickered in my mind, refusing to dim. The night stretched until dawn, dragging on with the cruel truth: I was already in way too deep, and I was drowning.#

The alarm blared, waking me up at my usual time of 7:30 am. My whole body felt freaked out and exhausted at the same time. Normally, 7:30 gave me plenty of time to start my day with breakfast and a shower before I had to open the shop at 9 a.m. It couldn't hurt to sleep in a little, especially when I was this tired. But then I remembered: Lea would be up early working on her shop with Randy and his crew.

The shower suddenly became a necessity.

As I rolled up the gates to my shop and turned on my open sign, I was somewhat relieved that Lea was nowhere to be seen. Maybe she was the type to sleep in? There was a part of me that felt a twinge of disappointment. Even though it was a Tuesday, it wasn't long before I had a steady stream of customers, needing everything from equipment to mount shelves to tools to unclog their own drains. I knew the second wouldn't go well and even encouraged the plumbing services we had in town, but some people were insistent on doing it themselves.

It was my lunch hour when I finally took a break. I had Bryce, one of my workers, a local college student, take over while I got myself some food. I could have gone upstairs and made a sandwich, but I wanted the fresh air. And I was curious about the progress on Lea's shop.

I headed out for lunch, trying to eye the flower shop the best I could while still heading to the diner. The lights were on, and there were multiple people working furiously inside. Had Lea hired a team to help get the shop ready before busy season? I shook my head. Did it really matter? She was supposed to be a one-night stand.

Lea

By the time I made it to the flower shop the next morning, Rick's was already bustling. Through the big front window, I could see him at the register, head bent slightly as he rang up a customer. He didn't see me, thankfully. I kept my head down and slipped through the flower shop's door, the old bell jingling softly behind me. The scent of aged wood and leftover potpourri still clung to the place, but soon, it would smell like fresh earth and green life.

Tonight was my last night at the inn. Tomorrow, my furniture—my life—would be arriving. Including the new bed I'd splurged on, a king-sized beast that promised me all the room I could want to sprawl out like a starfish. It was a small but meaningful rebellion against my old twin bed back at Mom's house, where I'd lived a little too long and slept a little too narrow. I loved living with her, but it was time for something that felt like mine.

Most of the other furniture I'd taken from Mom's. I wasn't ready to deal with emptying out my childhood home. I was here to try to start fresh. Yet, there was still a voice in the back of my head telling me I could run back to the city if it didn't work out.

A sudden clang at the back door made me jump. Randy had arrived—with a completely different crew than the day prior. I tried not to gape as they filed in behind him, but the part of me still adjusting to the realities of Hallow's Cove nearly short-circuited. First came someone who looked like a lizardman—except taller, broader, and definitely more dragon than gecko. Shimmering scales traced over his arms and peeked from under his high-visibility vest. Then came two others—hulking, tusked, greenish—and I couldn't tell if they were orcs or ogres or something else entirely. Lastly, a man who looked human, but only at a glance. His eyes were too reflective, like sunlight glinting off deep water, and his movements just a little too smooth.

I decided I'd ask Randy what they all were when we had a moment alone. I needed to figure out the right way to ask someone *what kind of monster are you* without sounding like a total jerk.

We'd finished the majority of the demolition the day prior—channeling all my rage and frustration about Rick had made me an excellent candidate for smashing things.

Today was going to be more demo and maybe starting with fresh drywall if we made good time.

"Ready for day two?" Randy asked with a grin, handing me a hard hat with a sticker that said Monsters Do It Better on it.

I took the hard hat, suppressing a laugh. "Always. Who's on the crew today?"

He motioned to the lizardman, who introduced himself as Gene. His handshake was strong enough to nearly pop my elbow from its socket. Gene's voice was unexpectedly gentle for a guy with a dorsal ridge and talons. "I'll handle structural. Randy says you want to keep the windows?"

I nodded. "If at all possible. I'll cry if they go."

Gene nodded approvingly. "Noted." He scribbled something in pencil on his forearm scales, then wandered off to measure the window frames.

The two orcs got to ripping up the last of the floor and muscled all the debris out back. The man with the deep-water eyes was apparently an electrician. He introduced himself as Caleb, then spent the next hour tracing every wire in the shop, muttering about "pre-ADA firetraps" and "code compliance nightmares." I liked Caleb immediately.

By noon, the crew had transformed the place. The old counter was gone, the floors stripped to pale, promising hardwood, the windows cleared and glowing with daylight. I'd taken a hundred photos on my phone to send to Britt, who replied in all caps: THIS IS GOING TO BE SO CUTE and then, in a second text, IM SO PROUD OF YOU. It was a little thing, but it buoyed my spirits.

Just before lunch, I decided I would take Maisie up on her offer to meet at Cool Beans. She said she didn't eat, but liked the vibe for working. It sounded like my kind of place.

"Hey, I'm heading out to meet someone, but you have my number, right?" I asked Randy, who was scribbling something on his clipboard while simultaneously holding a measuring tape with his teeth.

"Got it right here." He tapped the paper. "Go make friends. We'll take care of this."

Cool Beans was just a few blocks away from the shop and the inn, and the spring day had that soft, golden light that made the whole town look like a postcard. I still wasn't used to how walkable everything was here. No highways in sight. No traffic. Just slow, winding sidewalks lined with quaint shops and flickering lanterns.

When I arrived, I found Maisie already seated at the café table outside, her laptop open, fingers dancing across the keyboard. It hit me how much I needed this. Friends. A place. A real start. Britt was amazing but being here in Hallow's Cove made me realize how much I needed a life beyond my mom's flower shop.

The inside of Cool Beans always smelled like heaven—cinnamon, espresso, warm pastries, and the waitress at Ted's had been right. The first time I'd stopped by, I'd been expecting sticky plastic tables and a generic menu, but I couldn't have been more wrong. Cool Beans had a funky, eclectic mix of furniture, a sofa in the corner covered in patchwork throws, mismatched tables and chairs, and a display case full of monster-themed pastries like blood orange scones and tarts filled with black cherries and "witches' fingers." The chalkboard menu on the wall offered herbal teas with names like Ogre Away and Ghostly Ginseng. Cozy didn't begin to describe it. It felt like the kind of place that would ruin me for grocery store coffee forever, where regulars gathered daily, knowing exactly what they'd get with each visit.

I was scanning the menu, a bit overwhelmed by all the choices, when the cashier approached—and my brain momentarily short-circuited.

The man behind the counter was a wolf. Not a man with a beard. Not a guy in flannel with a scruffy vibe. A literal wolfman—tall, broad, covered in thick brown fur, with sharp eyes behind his glasses and a smile full of slightly too-long teeth. A little voice in my head said, *get a grip, this town is full of monsters,* but I wasn't ready for them to look so monstrous. And yet, he seemed completely at ease, like he didn't even know how out of place he'd be in any other café in any other town.

"Hey there," he said in a deep, pleasant voice that made me stand up straighter. "What can I get you?"

I blinked and, after a second of awkward silence, managed to stammer, "Um, iced vanilla latte and a lemon muffin, please."

He nodded, unfazed, moving with smooth, confident ease. No stares. No whispers. This was Hallow's Cove. He was normal here. I was the strange one for still getting starstruck, the only one who didn't know how to play it cool. I took a deep breath and resolved to stop gawking at every monster I saw. I headed back to Maisie just as the wolfman finished ringing me up.

When I slid into the seat across from her, Maisie looked up and smiled with a mix of warmth and mischief.

"Oh, good, you came!"

"Of course I did," I said, setting my bag down and trying to sound more sure of myself than I felt. "I told you I would."

"I know. But I thought maybe you'd get caught up at your store. Or, you know... chicken out because of Rick."

I groaned dramatically, sinking into my seat. "Let's not talk about him before I've had caffeine."

Maisie gave a knowing chuckle and shut her laptop, just as the wolfman returned with my order. He set it down gently in front of me, claws careful not to tear the paper cup.

"Hey, Mitch, this is Lea," Maisie said brightly. "The new flower shop owner."

"Nice to meet you!" Mitch's voice was warm and rumbly, perfectly matching his appearance. He offered his paw—er, hand—and I shook it. His claws were blunt, his grip firm. His palm was huge compared to mine. Like the rest of him, it seemed both untamed and inviting.

"Nice to meet you too." I hoped my smile didn't look too awestruck. I couldn't help it, he was the first wolven I'd met!

"Roan's over at the art center," Mitch added. "But if she swings back this way, I'll send her over."

I nodded, not entirely sure who Roan was, but eager to not seem like the new kid at school. Maisie seemed to have this whole town on a map; she knew everyone and everything. I'd have to catch up quickly if I wanted to keep pace with her, if I wanted to be more than a fleeting visitor.

I took my attention back to Maisie as Mitch left our table. She looked human sitting in front of me, but I knew she had lengthened canines hiding under her knowing smile.

"What?" I asked, as she continued to smirk at me. "Haven't gotten used to the monsters yet?" She laughed, nodding towards Mitch's retreating back.

I blushed. She'd noticed how flustered I was by the wolven.

"Well it was easy to get used to... Rick." I paused, feeling my face heat. "But they still catch me off guard when I'm not expecting it." My eyes flicked over to where the wolven barista was. I tried not to let them bug out of my head when I saw him helping a monster that appeared to be... a yeti? An abominable snowman? I realized I didn't know the difference between the two.

"You'll get used to it." She smiled kindly.

I put my head in my hands. "I should have really spent the weekend getting to know all the locals—rather than one local *really* well. What was I thinking going home with someone my first weekend here? How could I have thought I could have a breezy one-night stand and not run into him the next day? What a fucking moron."

"Hey, hey. You're used to life in the city where you can take someone from the bar home and never see them again—if you don't want to." She grabbed my hand to comfort me.

"Ugh. You're right. And he's so charming I was completely gone." I rolled my eyes at myself. Ridiculous.

"What are you going to do about it? You can't live next to him for the foreseeable future without doing something."

Maisie was right. I was going to have to talk to him. Just because we wanted vastly different things didn't mean we needed to be sworn enemies. We could be friendly neighbors.

Friendly neighbors who had one night of mind-blowing sex.

Chapter Eight

Lea

IT WAS EARLY EVENING when I decided to wash up and head out to Killy's. I'd spent the rest of the day deep cleaning my new apartment. It didn't need as much work as the shop, just a good clean and maybe some new fixtures down the line. My new bed and boxes had arrived, and I was grateful that the movers took care of the heavy lifting, allowing me to stay upstairs and direct them. I wasn't exactly *hiding* from Rick, but I didn't want to see him until I was ready.

I poked my head out of the shop to see if the coast was clear and headed toward the town bar. I had put on another dress. Jeans and a T-shirt were my regular go to, or most often, dirt-stained overalls, but I enjoyed dressing up and feeling girly every once in awhile.

I ordered a snakebite from the bar and surveyed the scene. It was much quieter on a weeknight, but there were still plenty of patrons. I zeroed in on Rick immediately. He was leaning against the bar, drink in hand, talking animatedly to a very pretty *human*. She was blonde and willowy. Tall and lean in a way I never would be. Jealousy surged in me, making me hot and flustered.

I'd come to Killy's to talk to Rick—we could at least agree to be civil. Yet here he was with someone else. Already. Maybe he was a new girl every night kind of guy. My stomach clenched at the idea of him having sex like that with someone else. I was torn between walking up to him and giving him a piece of my mind or quietly slinking away with my tail between my legs. I had already chewed him out in public once, I wasn't about to do it again. I was about to turn and leave, full drink still in hand, when Rick turned to see me.

Shit. So much for slinking away. I chewed my lip as Rick sauntered over, looking too good to be allowed.

"Lea," he said, almost casual, but not quite. There was something tight around his mouth and a flicker in his gold-flecked eyes that made me wish I'd spent an extra five minutes practicing my resting bitch face in the mirror.

"Rick." I let the word hang, hoping the weight would do some of the talking for me.

He glanced over his shoulder at the blonde, who was busy at the pool tables, and then back at me. "Didn't think I'd see you here tonight."

"Didn't think I'd see you with a plus-one so soon." There. That sounded pithy and not at all desperate. Success.

He winced, and I almost felt bad. "She asked for a lumber recommendation."

"I don't care if she asked for a damn house, Rick. You walked out of my bed like I was just another girl on your roster, and now I'm supposed to smile and watch you charm someone else like it doesn't hurt?" I hissed, loud enough for only him to hear.

Rick's jaw flexed. He looked away, then straight at me, eyes full of that weird, wounded patience I hated almost as much as I craved it. "Lea, what do you want from me?"

"Oh, I don't know," I shot back. "Maybe common decency?"

"So you want to just pretend it never happened and we're just neighbors? I can do that." His voice was low, meant only for me, and the words hit in that place just under the rib cage that never quite healed right.

I folded my arms, clutching the condensation-slick glass like a shield. "Yeah, maybe that's what I want. To pretend this never happened." I said, my tone revealing that couldn't be further from what I wanted.

Rick started to say something—maybe even something real, something I would remember and turn over in my head a thousand times later—but the blonde was suddenly at his elbow again, smiling up at him with a kind of easy, practiced charm that made me want to snap my glass against the bar and see if I could still remember how to use the jagged edge. She tucked a stray lock of hair behind her ear and then, with the oblivious confidence of someone who'd never had to work for attention, leaned into him and giggled at something he said that I couldn't even hear.

I was so done. The anger that had been simmering all day finally boiled up, scalding over my self-restraint. Before I could stop myself, I set my glass down with a thunk, all but slamming it onto the sticky surface of the bar, and turned on my heel.

The first few steps felt like walking out of my own skin, nerves zapping cold and electric up and down my arms. I could hear Rick behind me—not following, not calling out, just standing there, letting me go. Maybe that's what pissed me off the most: I stormed out like I wanted to be chased, but I wasn't sure if I wanted him to actually come after me or if I just wanted to prove I could leave first this time.

Rick

She stormed out, and I just stood there.

Fucking stood there, like a goddamn idiot.

The door slammed behind her, and the silence left in her wake was louder than any shouting match could've been. The woman I was talking to completely disappeared. I hadn't been lying. We were just talking shop. She happened to be in the wrong place at the wrong time. The few patrons at the bar who'd overheard turned back to their drinks, pretending they hadn't seen the whole thing unfold like some small-town soap opera.

I stared at the spot Lea been standing. The fire in her eyes, the crack in her voice, the way she'd looked at me like I'd broken something sacred.

Because I had.

And now she was gone. Probably packing up her things, figuring out the quickest way out of town, cursing herself for ever letting a minotaur between her legs—let alone near her heart.

Harley gave me a wary look as he slid another snakebite my way. I didn't even remember asking for it.

"You alright, Rick?" he asked, quieter than usual.

I didn't answer. Just stared down into the depths of the drink Lea had said was her favorite. She'd told me that story with this half-laugh, half-confession voice, like she'd already decided she wanted to trust me and couldn't quite stop herself.

I'd spent years playing it cool. Sleeping around. Keeping things light. Because the truth was, no one had ever made me feel seen. Not for who I was underneath the muscles and the horns and the player reputation. They wanted the idea of me. Not me.

But Lea... she looked at me like I was more. Like she was trying to figure out every hidden part of me without even realizing it. And it terrified the shit out of me.

Because I wanted her to figure me out. I wanted to let her in.

And now she thought I didn't give a damn.

I slammed back the rest of the drink and scrubbed a hand down my face. My pride was bleeding out all over the bar, but it wasn't just pride. It was fear. It was longing. It was the bitter, aching realization that I might have just met the only person I've ever really wanted something real with—and lost her before I even had a chance to try.

I left the bar by midnight, the old wound throbbing somewhere behind my sternum. The world felt too tight, the air too sharp. I didn't want to go home, so I let my feet carry me in slow, angry circles around Main Street. By the time I passed her window, the new shop was dark but not empty. I could see the faintest glow through the second-story glass, a silhouette moving behind the curtain. Lea, probably unpacking boxes or crying or both. My stupid heart did a little stutter-step at the idea.

I wanted her. There was no denying it. But I was also so fucking pissed—at her for lying, for the mess she'd made. I wanted to yell at her for it as much as I wanted to hold her again.

So I went to her.

I didn't think. Just turned on my heel and marched up the steps to her place, feeling the anger and heartache and fuck-it-all coil tight in my gut. The door to the shop was unlocked, boxes stacked high in the gloom. I took the stairs two at a time, every step vibrating the frame of the old building. At the top, I stopped. Raised my fist to knock. Lost my nerve, then knocked anyway—harder than I meant, loud enough to startle a banshee.

The door swung open, and there she was.

Lea stood in the half-light, curls natural, cheeks flushed, wearing a threadbare T-shirt and leggings. She looked so much herself it almost broke me. She was caught off guard, mascara faintly smeared from earlier, hands braced on the door.

"Rick," she said, voice low. "What the hell is going on?"

I stared at her. I didn't know if I wanted to yell or apologize, or collapse in her arms and let her fix every broken thing in me. For a second, I just stood there, breathing hard, the haze of Harley's cheap whiskey mixing with the hot mess of everything I'd been trying to tamp down for days. "I need to talk to you," I said, and even to my own ears it sounded raw.

She looked me up and down, eyes raking over my face and catching on the half-buttoned shirt, the smell of bar, the nervous tremor in my voice. She waited, arms crossed over her chest, daring me to do something—anything—besides stand there and glare.

I stepped inside. I half expected her to slam the door in my face, but she let it hang open, like she wanted an escape route, just in case. Maybe she did.

She beat me to the punch, her voice clipped. "If you're here to rub in that you've already moved on, don't bother. Message received, loud and clear." She folded her arms tighter, like she was keeping the rest of herself from leaking out.

The anger in me flared—instant, white-hot, and sharper than I meant. "You lied to me," I shot back. "Don't play hurt like I'm the asshole here. I thought you were

83

leaving. I gave you exactly what you asked for." My hands went to my hips.

Lea's eyes flashed, wounded and fierce all at once. "I never lied to you." She huffed, like she'd been holding that in all day. "And anyway, what was I supposed to do? Announce that I might actually want something real with you, after you made it very clear that you only do flings?" She held my gaze, and I could see her jaw tremble, even as her voice got stronger. "Would that have made it easier?"

"Yes!" I bellowed, and the echo came back at me off bare wood and drywall, rattling down the hallway. "You didn't think to maybe mention you bought the building next to mine?"

She laughed. "You think I came into this town with some master plan to trap you?"

"No—I don't know!" I shouted before I could stop myself. I realized I was pacing like a bull in a corral. I was standing right in front of her, so close I could see the flecks of green in her brown eyes.

For a second, neither of us moved. The air between us was electric—anger and longing and something else, something thicker, roping us together even as we both tried to break free.

She just shook her head, the movement small and precise. "You're not even sober," she said, her voice dropping to a near-whisper. "Come back when you are. Try using your words then, instead of just shouting."

That stopped me. For a second, I wanted to slam something—put my hand through drywall, smash the old light fixture over her head. Instead, I just stared at her, my jaw clenched so tight I could taste blood in the back of my mouth.

"I'm not drunk," I spat, but it was a lie. The whiskey haze made everything feel sharp and unfocused all at once.

"Don't come here if you're going to talk like that," she said, voice growing firmer. "If you want to yell at me, do it sober."

I blinked, head swimming. "I thought—"

"I don't care what you thought," she cut in. Her voice cracked, but her stance didn't waver. "I'm not going to discuss anything while you're this drunk. Not tonight. Maybe not ever."

Her apartment door clicked softly behind me, but its sound reverberated through my skull like a gunshot. I staggered up to the apartment, the stairs a crueler enemy than anything Lea could conjure. The night blurred in streaks of whiskey and regret, and by the time I collapsed onto the bed, I couldn't tell which was burning more.

Chapter Nine

Rick

THE SUN WAS FAR too bright when I woke up. It pierced through the curtains, slicing into my eyes and drilling straight through to the back of my head. For a moment, I thought I was back in Lea's bed at the inn. But the bed was empty, and the sheets were tangled around my legs. I lay there, groaning, wishing I could rewind everything to the moment before I'd fucked it all up—somehow knowing even with a fresh start I'd screw it all up again.

The hangover pelted me like a heavy summer thunderstorm, but the memory of her standing there, hurt and angry, was like going through a hurricane. Gravity became irrelevant. All I thought about was those eyes looking so disappointed in me, and my stomach roiled. I'd wanted to make things right. Instead, I'd shown up at her door, confirming every worst fear she had about me. I rolled over, burying my face in the pillow.

Fuck.

I peeled myself out of bed, the wooden floor too loud against hooves. I wasn't sure what to do. Give her space? Give her time? A part of me knew I should back off, let her decide if she wanted anything more to do with me. But another part—a bigger, more desperate part—wanted to go over there right now, sober and clear-headed, and try again.

I splashed cold water on my face and stared at my reflection. My shaggy hair was a mess, and regret had settled deep in my eyes. I needed to breathe. To think. To get my head on straight before I went to her again. Maybe I'd made an idiot of myself the night before, but she was still the one who got us into this situation.

The thought burned, but it also cleared the haze. I wasn't just going to let her waltz into town, wreck my head, and then sweep out again. If she wanted to play games, she'd picked the wrong minotaur.

I stormed out of the apartment, down to the shop. I didn't know what I'd say when I saw her, but I knew one thing: I wasn't going to be the one to retreat in embarrassment.

I knocked on the flower shop door once, hard. No answer. The windows were covered in brown paper, but I could hear music blasting—early 2000s, some boy band—leaking through the cracks.

I didn't wait for an invitation. I turned the handle and stepped inside.

It was an explosion of color—fresh paint, stacks of packaging, pots of flowers in various states of bloom. Lea stood behind the counter, her curls piled up with two pencils and a spade jammed through them like it was a hairdo straight from an art supply riot. Lea was hunched over her phone, typing one-handed, the other hand holding a half-eaten donut.

She didn't look up.

"Lea." I called over the music.

"Rick?" Her voice was startled, then cutting. "Sobered up, have you?" She turned down the old-fashioned CD player she had next to her.

She was right, but it still stung."Yeah, I have. And if you are going to stay here, then we need to at least be civil to each other."

Her tone was pure steel. "Fine. Let's be civil neighbors." She set down the donut with a deliberate lack of care, wiped her fingers on a rag, and gave me a glare that could scour rust off metal.

"Run your shop. I'll run mine. We'll keep it professional." Her laugh was sharp-edged but real. "You think you can manage that, big guy?"

I bristled at the word. "Careful," I said, stepping closer.

"Or what?" she said, chin up, lips twitching. "You'll mope at me? Glare holes in my drywall?"

"Don't push me," I said, but it came out hoarse, barely more than a growl.

The look she gave me then—defiant, electric—should have been a warning. Instead, it detonated every rational thought in my skull. With no more than a heartbeat's hesitation, I leaned forward, flattening my palms on the counter. She didn't recoil. She didn't even blink. She just stared me down, chest rising and falling like she was daring me to cross the line.

So I did.

In one motion I vaulted the counter, scattering the screws and nails that Randy had left behind, landing just inches from her. She didn't flinch. If anything, she squared her shoulders, tilting her chin up so our faces were even. I could see the spark in her eyes, a riot of hurt and want and willful, impossible hope.

"Didn't think you had it in you," she whispered, and the words barely made it past her lips before I crushed my mouth into hers. She met the kiss like a slap, hard and greedy. There was nothing polite about it. All lips and tongue and an angry, desperate gasp that burned in my mouth. Her hands tangled in my shirt, bunching the fabric, and she yanked me so close I could have sworn she meant to tear me in half. Good. Maybe I wanted her to.

I pressed her back into the wall behind the counter, feeling every point of contact: her small fingers digging into the flesh of my shoulders, her thighs bracing my hips, the fever-hot pulse pounding in her throat as my lips trailed down to claim it. She let out a sound—not quite a moan, not quite a growl, but something feral—and the need in it made me lose the last shreds of sense I had.

My hands roamed over her, everywhere, gripping her hips, sliding up her back, tangling in her hair. I wanted every part of her, wanted to erase the distance we'd carved between us. I kissed down her neck, feeling her shiver against me, feeling the heat between us grow until it was more than I could handle. Until I was hard and aching and ready to take her right there on the shop floor, to show her how much I wanted her, how much she meant.

"Upstairs," she panted, her voice urgent.

I pulled back, breathless, my eyes searching hers for something—anything—to tell me this was real.

Her gaze was steady, and she tugged at my hand, leading us through the mess of paint cans and empty boxes and up the stairs to her apartment.

Lea

My pulse throbbed in my ears, the sharp hammering of my heart matching the wild scramble of our feet as I hauled him up the stairs. We were a frantic mess of tangled limbs and reckless urgency, my boots and his hooves sending vibrations through the old wood, the soft glow of midmorning light be damned. I didn't know if this was madness or desperation, and I didn't give a fuck. I needed him, needed the heat of him, needed that first kiss—searing, possessive, branding my soul.

I kicked open the apartment door. Rick was mine the second he stumbled inside, his mouth crashing onto mine, fierce, demanding, tasting of stale whiskey, sleep, and a primal hunger that matched my own. I drank him down like the strongest shot, body already yearning for more, already aching for every part of him.

"Lea." He groaned my name, ragged and raw, like a plea and a challenge rolled into one.

I tore at his shirt, buttons flying, fingers clumsy, frantic in their need. He grabbed my waist and slammed me against the wall, heat and desperation in every movement. I locked my legs around him, feeling the hard, urgent length of him press between my thighs. Everything about him was molten, insistent. His fingers dug into my hips, anchoring me to him as he ground into me, his breath hot and heavy on my neck.

He crushed my lips again. My nails scored fiery lines down his back, pulling a low, feral moan from deep in his chest. The sound resonated through me, echoed straight to my core, told me how much he needed this too. I writhed, gripping him with my thighs as he carried me to the sheet-draped bed, still warm from the morning sun. The gentleness with which he laid me down was a stark contrast to the storm in his eyes.

I whimpered at the lack of contact. But he was on me again, in an instant, hands and mouth frantic, unzipping my jeans, tugging both pants and underwear off in one quick motion, leaving me bare beneath him. He licked a clear, torturous path from my hipbone to my inner thigh. I bucked, arching as his teasing tongue circled my clit, sending jolts of electricity through me. Fingers tangled in his hair, I pulled him deeper. He growled into me, the vibration electric and more intense than I could stand.

He latched onto my clit, sucking hard, and I nearly screamed. I didn't care if the whole building heard. No part of me wanted to play coy, not with him, not right now. His hands pinned my hips, huge and unyielding, holding me open while he licked into me, tongue flat and greedy, flicking up and down like he'd been starving for this, for me. I clenched around the emptiness, wanting more, and he must have read my mind because he slipped two thick fingers inside, curling them perfectly, hitting that sweet, pulsing spot.

"Shit, Rick," I gasped, slamming my fist into the mattress, "don't stop, don't you fucking dare—"

He growled, low, and pulled back just long enough to say, "I love how you taste. How you fall apart for me. Let go. I want to feel you come." His voice was thick and hungry, and I nearly snapped in half hearing him say it.

"Please," I begged, so far gone I barely recognized my own voice.

He answered by pushing in a third finger, a stretch that burned so good I saw stars. His tongue kept circling my clit, relentless, coordinated with the curl of his hand. He murmured against me, "That's it. Let yourself go. Give it to me, all of it. I want to taste you when you come."

I cried out and he only doubled down, fucking me with his hand, sucking my clit until my body detonated. Release poured through me, hot and uncontrollable, my whole body shuddering and clamping down on his fingers. He groaned, delighted, and kept going, drawing every last spasm out of me until I was a limp, trembling wreck on the sheets. Then he climbed up and kissed me, hard, I tasted myself on his tongue and moaned into his mouth.

He was out of his jeans in seconds and I didn't hesitate in wrapping my hand around him, marveling again at the sheer size and the impossible feel of him. He sucked in a breath, his body tensing, and I pulled him to me, greedy for the fullness, the pressure, the absolute ruin of it.

He knelt between my thighs, angling himself against my entrance, and just the blunt head of his cock had me arching off the bed, clutching at his arms. He gripped my knees, spreading me wide, and pushing in all the way in one stroke, a heat and stretch that bordered on pain but somehow edged into pleasure.

For a moment, he stayed still, buried fully, letting us both feel the tight, liquid heat of him inside. His eyes, dark and tender, searched mine for permission.

"You okay?" he whispered, voice rough and strained.

"God, yes." The words spilled out in a moan as I slid my legs around his hips, tugging him deeper, urging him to move.

And move he did. Slow, deep strokes that sent stars exploding behind my eyelids. I gripped the sheets, heels digging into his back, urging him faster, harder. He obeyed, rocking into me with mounting speed, every thrust a crash of pleasure. My breath caught, chest heaving like a wild animal as he shifted angles, lifting one knee so his cock brushed my G-spot just right. Fire exploded inside me; I clamped down, my body convulsing around him.

His groan, raw and guttural, echoed off the bare walls. Wetness pooled between us, bodies slick with sweat and desperation. I was so close.

"Don't stop," I begged, voice trembling on the brink. "Please—"

Rick growled and obeyed, pounding into me with a ferocity that sent the bed crashing against the wall. Our gasps and moans mingled with the distant hum of morning traffic, a symphony of raw, primal need. Then I shattered—heat surging from belly to spine, nails digging into his shoulders as I rode the tremors.

Rick followed seconds later, his cum filling me up, heat dribbling down the inside of my legs. He collapsed, heavy and spent, chest rising and falling against mine. We lay tangled, sweat cooling on our skin, hearts hammering in unison, breaths ragged and syncopated.

We stayed that way until the blood stopped roaring in my ears and I remembered how to breathe again. Rick's head was tucked into the curve of my neck, his horns scraping the drywall, his arms a band of iron around my waist.

Eventually, I found my voice. "If this is your version of talking things out," I rasped, "it's wildly effective, but I think I missed half the conversation."

He laughed, the sound raw. "Gimme a sec. My brain isn't... working right now." He rolled off me, giving me just enough space to breathe, but still holding on like he thought I might float away.

I closed my eyes, head spinning, and let the silence fill up the cracks in me. For the first time since the night we met, neither of us had anything to hide behind.

Rick was the one who broke first. He drew a shaky breath, voice husky but clear as he said, "I'm sorry I left."

I stared up at the ceiling, letting the words settle, my brain working slow and strange. He said it like it hurt, like the words had been pulled out of some deep, secret place. I waited for the rest of the sentence—but he just lay there, holding me, breathing like he was afraid I'd vanish if he let go.

I tried to swallow the lump in my throat, and found myself answering without thinking. "I'm sorry I lied," I said. "I just... I thought if I kept it light, then I wouldn't get disappointed. I wouldn't get hurt." I laughed, a small, bitter sound. "Guess that worked out well for both of us, huh?"

He grunted, then, with a gentleness that undid me, rolled onto his side, propping himself up on one elbow. He stared at me, like he was memorizing the landscape of my face. "You want to try again?" he asked.

Not a joke, not a dare. Just that simple, terrifying question.

When he brushed a stray curl from my forehead, carefully, like he was afraid he'd frighten it back into hiding, I couldn't say anything except, "Yeah. I do."

His smile was crooked, almost shy. "We could start over. For real. Do it right this time." He tucked the sheet around our waists, as if the thin cotton could shield us from the mess of the last few days. "We could go on a date. Like normal people."

I snorted. "I'm not sure there's a universe where we're normal people."

He grinned, showing his brilliant flat white teeth. "I think we can manage a normal date."

We lay there, the absurdity of it sinking in—two idiots who couldn't go a single day without detonating each other's emotional landmines. But somehow, the idea of starting over felt less terrifying in the aftermath of mutual destruction. Like maybe, once all the bullshit was burned away, we could build something honest on the ashes.

"Okay," I said finally, the word fragile but true. "We start over." I reached for his hand, weaving my fingers through his. "But I'm warning you now: I'm horrible at first dates. I get nervous and say dumb things and usually spill something on myself."

Rick squeezed my hand, the pressure nearly cracking my knuckles, but in a nice way. "Spilling things is fine. I stain everything I wear within five minutes. Occupational hazard." He paused, looking suddenly nervous. "Uh, so, I know we said we're starting over—like, emotionally—but..." He trailed off, biting his lower lip, which frankly only made him look less intimidating and more like an overgrown teen at his first school dance. "Does that mean we have to wait for, um, physical stuff?"

I burst out laughing. "Are you asking if we can have sex while we're dating like normal people?"

He bit his lip and looked anywhere but my face, obviously embarrassed. This was an odd convo, especially considering we were still lying naked together.

"I mean, not every day. Unless you want to," he blurted. "Or you don't want to. You set the pace, I just—" He stopped, then added miserably, "I'm real bad at waiting."

I kept laughing, the endorphins and oxytocin and whatever else made a person feel safe and stupid and good turning me into a human giggle-loop.

"You're adorable, you know that?" I said, touching the side of his face, watching him go pink at the compliment.

"I'm not," he protested, which made it even better, because he was. "I'm, like, objectively not."

"Objectively, you're a minotaur with a heart and a very, very magnificent—" I cut myself off, blushing for the first time in years. "Never mind."

He cocked a brow and gave a wolfish smile that I was pretty sure he practiced in the mirror when no one was watching. "If you're referring to my equipment, you could just say it. I know I'm not human, after all. Biological advantages and all that." He said it with a mix of pride and bashfulness that made my insides go warm and loose.

"I prefer the phrase 'superior craftsmanship,'" I deadpanned, and his laugh was a deep, full-body thing that shook the mattress and made me giggle in spite of how ridiculous we both were.

We spent the next hour sprawled out and aimless, playing a game of gentle one-upmanship: who could tell the dirtiest joke, who could do the worst celebrity impression, who could come up with the best fake name for the new shop. He suggested *From Seed to Sorrow* with such earnestness that I almost believed him, and then collapsed into helpless laughter when I threatened to commission a neon sign.

Eventually we both drifted off, exhausted from the events of the past few days.

Chapter Ten

Rick

I WOKE UP IN her bed, sunlight knifing past the old curtains and dappling my skin with gold. It was too warm and too soft, the mattress springy in that way only a brand-new bed could be. For a split second, disoriented and dumb, I could've sworn it was my own place—until the scent of Lea hit me, honest and human and bright as a bouquet. I blinked, working the last of sleep from my eyes.

Lea was sprawled beside me, half-buried in the quilt, her curls a halo of wild around her face. She slept with her mouth open, arm thrown across my chest, drooling a little in the corner, and I'd never seen anything so perfect. The sun picked out the freckles on her shoulder.

I watched her chest rise and fall, steady but shallow. It took a minute to realize her hand was still on my heart, fingers splayed and perfectly still, as if she needed to make sure it kept beating. I smiled at the thought, then, unable to help myself, brushed a single curl from her cheek. Her nose scrunched and she made a noise, swatting at my hand like a bug, but didn't wake up.

It was well past noon. The light was deeper, fuller, the sort that made you think you'd slept through a whole season instead of just a few hours.

She roused gradually, grumbling into the pillow, then blinked at me with bleary suspicion. "You're still here?" she croaked, voice full of sleep and surprise. "I was half-convinced you'd Houdini again."

I snorted, tucking my head into the pillow to hide how much it stung. "I don't plan on running this time," I said, softer than I meant to.

She propped herself up on one elbow, surveying me with a mixture of skepticism and something warmer. "Good," she said, and the word glowed in my chest. "Because if you did, I'd have to tell the entire downtown that you cry after sex. And not in a cute way."

I barked a laugh, rolling toward her. "You wouldn't."

She leveled a finger at me. "Try me. I'm already on a first name basis with the coffee shop and two-thirds of the construction crew. I have more social firepower than you think."

I considered this, then rolled onto my back, fingers laced behind my head, and let her enjoy her victory. "I surrender," I said. "But if you're going to destroy my reputation, at least let me buy you a real dinner first."

She snorted, then eyed me warily. "Are you asking me on a date?"

I tried to play it cool, but my throat tightened. "Yeah. I am. A real one. Not just..." I gestured vaguely at the bed and the tangle of limbs and sheets that was our entire relationship history. "Not just this."

The silence stretched. She chewed her lip, thinking, and I wondered if I'd misread everything. But then she rolled closer, curls spilling across my chest, and grinned that crooked, vulnerable grin I was coming to crave.

"So what did you have in mind? Candlelight? Moonlit stroll through the cemetery? Or just a couple of burgers at the diner, with extra fries and a milkshake with two straws?" She feathered her fingers along my shoulder—teasing, tentative.

I fought a smile, letting her think she'd stumped me. "We could start basic: burgers and milkshake, like you said. Then work our way to moonlit cemetery strolls once I'm sure you won't stake me in the heart and steal my keys."

She snorted. "Please. If I was going for heart or keys I would've done it last night." The words sounded light, but her fingers curled possessively over my chest. "Besides, I like you with your heart intact." Her voice dipped, the joke almost trembling at the edge. "It looks good on you."

We fell quiet, a new kind of hush threading between us. The sunlight on her face made her look different—tender and sleepy, every line soft and unfinished. I wanted to reach out and press her into my life, make her a part of it.

"I'll pick you up?"

She looked up, a little shy. "Yeah. Tomorrow. Seven?"

I nodded, drinking in her face, the upward flick of her mouth, the fringe of her lashes. She pecked me once, feather-light, like a promise.

"Now go," she whispered, pushing at my chest. "I have to get the rest of these boxes unpacked. And if you're here, I'll just keep distracting myself with your... face."

"Face, huh?"

"Or other parts. Don't get cocky."

I left, finally, with a dumb grin and a saunter in my steps even Randy would pick up on.

Lea

I spent the rest of the day and early evening unpacking and blissed out on my unexpected morning with Rick. I went to bed early, tired from multiple days of an emotional rollercoaster back-to-back. When I woke, it was with a start—my phone vibrating violently against the cheap bedside table, a harpy shriek of ringtone I'd assigned to Britt years ago. My body still hummed with the aftershock of Rick, but the rest of me had gone stiff and sore, as if sleep had decided to punish me for exerting myself. I groped blindly for the phone, knocking it to the floor in the process, then rolled out of bed and answered it on the second ring, voice croaky.

"Jesus, Britt, what time is it?"

"Eight-thirty," she fired back, all clipped vowels and caffeine. "Have you been murdered yet?"

"Not unless this counts as an out-of-body experience," I muttered, flopping back onto the mattress and drawing the sheet over my eyes. "What's up?"

"I called you three times last night. You went missing from our scheduled debrief. Are you being held against your will by hunky monsters?" She dropped her voice to a stage whisper. "Or did you finally get some?"

I laughed, but it came out more like a whimper. "You don't want the details, trust me. My body is in recovery mode. I can barely walk."

"Oh, I want every detail. But that's not why I'm calling." There was a pause, the sound of her breathing. "I wish I could say it was a social call, but I've got some bad news."

The shift in her tone was like a cold hand up my spine. I sat up, fully awake now, clutching the sheet to my chest. "What happened?"

"A pipe burst at the shop," Britt said. "I got a call from the building manager this morning. Flooded the whole back room and at least half the storeroom. I went over there and the place was a swamp. It looks... bad, Lea. It looks like we lost most of the seed inventory, too. The new stuff you ordered for spring? Floated off like tiny, expensive rafts." Britt's voice tried for lightness, but there was a tremor under it. "I know you left the city to get away from this kind of bullshit, but I don't think we have a choice. Building management is saying you have to come back for a look—your name is on the deed."

The words knocked the breath right out of me. I stared at the ceiling, the patch where new paint met old, and tried to picture the shop underwater—my mother's counters warped and peeling, buckets of seeds and bulbs dissolved to useless mush. I'd left everything in decent order so I wouldn't have to look back, and now it wanted me, like some ancient, needy ghost.

"Lea?" Britt's voice was gentler now, the way it got whenever one of us needed to cry at work and didn't want anyone else to see. "Are you okay?"

I took a slow breath. My heart was a sodden lump, but I could hear my mother's voice—her real one, not the cheap imitation my memory liked to play when I was feeling weak—saying, "It's just stuff, baby. Stuff can be fixed." I wanted to believe that, but I also felt the loss in my marrow. That shop had been my mom's entire world. It had been mine, too, for longer than I cared to admit.

I cleared my throat, forcing my voice to steady. "Yeah. I'm okay. I'll, uh, come back and look at it. Let them know I'll be there tonight or first thing tomorrow."

"Are you sure?" Britt whispered, as if she already knew the answer.

Around the room, boxes crowded the walls, cutting unfamiliar shapes out of sunlight. It was nothing like the old shop. I thought about the wreckage waiting for me, the memory of my mom in every water-logged splinter. But I also thought of what Maisie said, about surviving one life only to start another. I could do this. I had to.

"No, I need to see it myself," I said. "I'll get on the road as soon as I get dressed."

I threw on clothes—yesterday's shirt, clean enough, and my softest jeans, the ones with the paint flecks and a rip in the knee from when I'd tried to move a dresser alone. I didn't bother with makeup or my usual braid; I just pulled my hair back into a poof and silk scarf and jammed my feet into battered sneakers. I grabbed my wallet, keys, and a granola bar, and was halfway out the door when I realized I hadn't called Rick. We were supposed to go on our first date that night—or our first redo date.

I found his number—he'd entered it in my phone as "Rick (Hardware, Minotaur, Hot)"—and pressed call before I could overthink it. It rang twice before he answered, voice already awake but husky.

"Hey, Lea," he said, and I heard him smile into the phone. "Was just thinking about you."

I almost lost it right there. "That's sweet. Listen, something came up. I have to go back to the city for a day, maybe two."

I braced myself for a joke, a quip, something to detach us from the awkward intimacy of actually needing each other. But all he said was, "Are you okay?"

"I'm fine. I just... it's a long story. Can I tell you when I get back?"

He made a contemplative noise, then: "You want company?"

It was the last thing I expected, and I almost said yes, even though the idea of showing him the ruin of my old life made me feel naked and exposed. "I think this is something I need to do on my own."

"Yeah." He waited, giving me a full five seconds to change my mind, his voice softer than I'd ever heard it. "I get that. You know where to find me when you're back?"

I could see him in my head, broad-shouldered and still a little awkward, pacing a hardware aisle or hunched over a cup of black coffee. I wanted to reach through the phone and grab on, but instead I just said, "Yeah. Don't go anywhere, okay?"

"I won't. Promise."

I let myself believe it. Then I hung up, squared my shoulders, and headed for the car.

Chapter Eleven

Lea

THE DRIVE TO THE city felt endless, a slow crawl through mist and uncertainty. I tried to focus on the road, the skyline, anything other than the pounding questions in my head.

My hands were shaking by the time I found parking outside the shop. It was cold, drizzly, the sidewalk slick with a thin film of ice and city grime. I stood in front of the door for a full minute, just staring at the peeling gold letters on the glass—THOMPSON & DAUGHTER—a little smudged but still legible. Britt was waiting inside, face pinched and eyes red-rimmed. She'd beaten me by an hour, probably, and had already picked up coffee and a box of donuts, like she could bribe the universe into giving us a softer landing.

The bell over the door still jingled when I stepped in, but it was a pitiful sound, like the whole building had caught a cold. The air inside was a punch: mildew and scorched electrical, the sharp tang of rotted wood and wet, ancient carpet. My sneakers squished as I walked. The floor behind the register, once soft and faded from years of standing, was buckled and warped, a sea of blistered laminate undulating under each step. The counter—my mother's counter, the one I'd sat behind and traced names into with a ballpoint pen while she did payroll—was bloated and stained, rising at the seams like a corpse.

Britt stood in the wreckage, untouched cup of coffee in her hands, and tried for a smile. She wore her old work boots and the green hoodie she'd lifted from the soccer team in college, and the sight of her in that uniform almost did me in.

"Welcome home," she said, voice hoarse, and I just nodded, because there was nothing left in my own throat.

We moved quietly, surveying the damage. The storeroom was the worst. The shelves had collapsed, spilling a sodden rainbow of packets and seed tins into the water that still pooled ankle-deep. My boots quickly soaked through, the icy chill climbing up my calves before I even reached the back wall. The inventory—months, maybe years of it—was useless now. I picked up a fistful of seeds, once so carefully counted and catalogued, now washed to a clump of mulch in my palm. My mother's neat handwriting on the labels was smudged, the ink bleeding out like the memory of her voice.

I sank onto a crate near the ruined shelving, brittle plastic giving way a little under my weight, and let my head drop into my hands. I'd braced for this on the drive over. I'd told myself it was all just stuff. I knew that, and it didn't matter. Everything here was haunted, and now it was rot, all the history blurring into a sopping, ruined mess.

Britt crouched beside me, her usual armor of sarcasm gone. She didn't reach for me, just sat, mirroring my posture, squinting into the same dark corners I was studying. "It sucks," she said at last, with a kind of reverence, like she didn't want to break the spell of the silence. "I was hoping it'd be less bad, but, uh. Nope. Just garden-variety apocalypse."

I coughed out a laugh, surprised to find I still had one in me. She smiled at that, a real, small thing, and then rested her chin on her knees, huddled in against the cold and wet.

"I guess we'll have to pull everything," Britt said, surveying the ragged remains of the back room. "Drywall, shelving, the whole nine yards. And the insurance guy is coming at two. Just so you know."

I tried to answer, but my voice had gone sticky again, too weighted down with grief and mess to say anything. I picked at a loose thread on my jeans and stared at the warped ceiling tile above, counting the slow drip of the brownish water that still leaked, weeping for what it once was.

Through that haze, I heard Britt get up, boots squelching, then come back with a couple of towels from the front closet. She draped one over my shoulders before wrapping herself in the other, pulling it tight like a cocoon. "Look, we're gonna need at least a dozen fans and maybe a priest to exorcise the place," she said, voice dry but kind. "But we'll get through it." She nudged my knee with hers. "You want to crash at my place tonight? No way in hell you're fit to stay at your mom's house, and I made up the guest room. It's got blackout curtains and a weighted blanket. I even bought you the fancy oat milk."

I tried to say no, tried to insist that I was fine, but the last twenty-four hours had left me hollowed out, running on pure survival and muscle memory. "Yeah," I said, the word as limp as my spine. "I don't want to be alone tonight."

Britt's mouth went soft at the edges, a comfort I hadn't realized I was looking for. "You're never alone, you idiot." She slid her arm around my shoulders, holding on just long enough that I could feel her pulse, her warmth, the stubborn thrum of life that refused to be drowned by the mess.

The insurance guy arrived precisely at two, with a clipboard and a bureaucratic frown. By the time he left, the shop was colder, darker, and I was shivering. Britt locked the front door and turned to me with a look that said she'd carry me if she had to. Instead, she just made me stand and follow her out to her car—the ancient, rusted Corolla that had ferried us to college and back a hundred times. It smelled like old coffee and lemon air freshener, and as she cranked the heater, I let the hum lull me into the closest thing to peace I'd felt all day.

At her place—a cozy, second-floor walk-up above a laundromat—she hustled us inside and turned on every lamp, banishing the gloom. I barely remembered to unlace my boots before collapsing onto her couch, towel still wrapped like a shroud around my shoulders. Britt set water to boil, then rummaged in her cabinet for the chamomile tea I hated, but which my mom had always insisted on in times of crisis. I almost cried again just seeing the blue box.

"Take your time," Britt said from the kitchen. "We don't have to talk about it right now."

I nodded, staring at my knees, wrung out and raw. The tea was steeping when she returned, the mug pressed between my hands. I could barely feel the heat, but the gesture landed. We sat side by side in the hush, and it was only after I'd drained half the mug that Britt finally asked, "Are you going to stay in the city, or head back to Hallow's Cove?"

The question was soft, but it cracked open the tremor I'd been holding on to for hours.

"I don't know," I whispered, cheeks burning. "I need to stay here and fix this—but I am knee deep in demo of the shop in Hallow's Cove. I can't be both places at once. I don't know what to do. I feel split in two..." I trailed off pathetically.

Britt made a tsk sound. "You don't have to decide today. Just get through the next five minutes, and then the next, and the next. Hell, I'll stage a sit-in if insurance gives you any more grief. I'm still flexible from yoga class."

It was supposed to make me laugh, and it almost did.The next morning, I rose early. While I hadn't figured out long term, I couldn't leave Britt and the shop as it was. It wasn't her responsibility. We spent the next two days in a fog of triage. Britt made it her mission to salvage whatever we could: old photos, a handful of undamaged books, the battered sign from the window. I called the plumber, the insurance rep, the disaster cleanup crew, and my landlord, and tried to sound like a person who had their shit together. The shop emptied out box by box, the shelves stripped bare and left to warp in the cold. I boxed up the smallest things that mattered: a tin of my mother's favorite tea, a bundle of dried lavender she'd hung from the ceiling, a handful of polaroids from the first year I worked there after college. The rest was junk by comparison, a loss I could live with. But the rest—the history, the love, the literal blood and sweat—was gone.

That night, I lay awake in Britt's guest room, limbs heavy, brain picking over the wreckage with the slow, endless precision of a forensic accountant. I kept thinking about what Maisie said, about how you do all the things you put off once death has stripped away your excuses. I tried to imagine my mother, hands on her hips, surveying the mess and deciding it was time to start over. She'd probably crack a joke about biblical floods, then make me sweep out the mud while she called the neighbors to see who wanted sopping packets of discount nasturtiums.

I missed her so much. The absence was a living thing, clawing at my insides. I wondered if it was stupid to miss her more now, when she'd been gone for months, than in the first weeks after her funeral. Maybe because before, I had been so busy keeping the shop above water—literally and figuratively—that there hadn't been time for grief to get its hooks in so deep. Now, with nothing left but the bones of her life and my own empty hands, the loss felt fresh all over again.

The next morning, Britt was up early, boiling eggs and lining up phone calls with the precision of an air traffic controller. She pressed a cup of coffee into my hands, then nudged me toward the shower with a gentle, bossy hand. "You're not going to solve everything before lunch," she said. "But you can put on clean underwear and eat breakfast like a human being."

I did as told, sitting in the puddle of sunlight that spilled through Britt's kitchen window, and let her mother me. For the first time since the call, I felt a little less like a ghost haunting my own life. I made it through two eggs and half a banana before the silence got uncomfortable.

I pushed away from the table and wandered into the living room. The city morning was muffled: a constant, distant hum of traffic, the occasional siren, the slow, predatory prowl of the garbage truck. I checked my phone—no new messages. No calls from Rick.

I hated that I hoped for one even though I told him I needed to do this on my own.

Quietly, I left Britt's apartment and walked the ten familiar blocks to my mom's old house. It stood at the end of a dead-end street, a pale yellow two-story with a crooked mailbox and a porch swing that still creaked in a breeze. I'd spent my whole life in this house, every inch of it mapped into the muscles of my body. I unlocked the front door and stood in the entryway, letting the heavy smell of old air and lemon cleaner hit me in the face. I still didn't know what I was going to do, but I knew I wasn't going to be able to leave the city without addressing the house I grew up in.

Nothing had changed. Her shoes were still lined up in the entry, practical and well-worn. Coats hung in the closet, including one I'd outgrown a decade ago but she refused to donate because "it made me look collegiate." The living room was set for the ghost of a party, the runner on the table pressed crisp and flat. I walked from room to room, checking for ghosts, finding only the same aching stillness. In my old bedroom, the twin bed was made tight, complete with hospital corners just as my mother had taught me. I opened the closet, half-expecting to see some relic of my childhood—a box of graded papers, an old soccer trophy—but it was empty, except for a single wire hanger and a forgotten scarf.

I sat on the bed, hands folded in my lap, and tried to think of some reason to stay. There was comfort in the familiarity, in the way the air bent around me, settling in all the old grooves. But it didn't feel like home anymore. It felt like a place I'd already left, like a chapter I'd reread so many times the pages had gone thin.

The plan, originally, was to rent out the house—to hold it as an escape hatch, a safety net if the flower shop in Hallow's Cove failed. But now, surrounded by the echo of my mother's life, I knew that was a lie.

I wasn't coming back. I'd changed more in the last week than in the past year of mourning, and the idea of folding myself back into this house—of pretending the old patterns still fit—made me feel sick and small.

I was going to have to sell it. Not yet, maybe, but soon. The thought was brutal, but right. I needed the money if I was going to fix up the shop in the city, if I was going to have a chance at making the Hallow's Cove thing work. The logical, adult part of me wondered why I hadn't come to this conclusion months ago, but the rest of me—the soft, stubborn, petulant daughter—still clung to the memory of my mom's hands on my shoulders, telling me I'd always have a home to come back to even after she was gone. I let myself cry for her, for the house, for every ugly and beautiful thing that had ever happened under this roof. The tears felt cleaner this time, more final—like a storm that, when it passed, left the sky clearer than before.

Chapter Twelve

Rick

I DIDN'T HEAR FROM Lea for three days. Which, after the way things ended, was maybe fair, maybe the new normal. I tried not to be the guy who kept texting, who sent a running tally of "just checking in"s and "hey, you okay?"s. I tried to be the guy who kept his word, who gave her the breathing room I thought she needed.

But I was a liar and a hypocrite, and by the time her silence hit the seventy-two-hour mark, I was already inventing reasons to walk past the flower shop, just to see if the lights were on.

They weren't. Not once. Not even in the middle of the night, when I left my own apartment with the excuse of midnight inventory, and stood on the sidewalk with my hands jammed in my jacket pockets, watching for a flicker behind her windows. At first, I told myself she was sleeping late, or working in the back, or maybe—just maybe—burying herself in whatever project she'd dreamed up to make the place feel like hers. But as each hour ticked by, that hope shrank, replaced by something sour and restless in my gut.

On the fourth morning, I lost the battle with my self-respect and called her. Straight to voicemail. I hung up before the beep, then slammed my phone on the counter. It wasn't just nerves anymore. It was anger, low and smoldering, the kind that made my pulse throb in my temples and my hands clench into fists for no reason at all.

I grabbed my keys, shoved them into my pocket, and called to Bryce. "You're running the shop today," I barked, the clipped intensity of my voice making him jump. "I've got to go."

I drove. Not fast, not reckless. Just the steady, single-minded way you do when there's nothing else you can do. I stopped at the city's edge, just before the bridge, and sat in the idling truck like a statue, wondering if this counted as stalking or saving.

There was a moment where I saw myself, really saw myself: a minotaur in a battered Ford, halfway to the city for a woman who might not even want him there, a woman who might already be packing up her failures and moving on, leaving Hallow's Cove (and me) the way she found it. Fuck it. I was going after her. I wasn't letting her leave without seeing what could have been. I wasn't going to let this slip out of my hands again.

I drove, and the city took me like a punch. I parked outside her shop, not even caring about the expired meter or the glare of a meter maid. The doors to the place were propped open, air thick with the smell of mold and wet sawdust. I ducked inside, ready for anything except what I found.

Lea was nowhere in sight. A woman I didn't recognize was there, standing on a half-collapsed milk crate and taping off a ruined section of drywall with hazard-yellow caution tape. She wore cut-off jeans, a shirt that said "Plants Before People"—she had to be Lea's best friend Britt.

The second she saw me, her eyebrows went up. "Well, well. If it isn't the minotaur of the moment," she said, stepping down off the crate and landing with a wet squelch. "If you're here to sell us a dehumidifier, you're about three days late."

The place was in shambles—no, worse. I'd seen post-flood basements in better shape. The walls were peeling, ceiling drooping with water weight, shelves buckled and vomiting ruined packets of seeds. Puddles reflected the chaos, and the air stank of dead things: mold, mildew, memories.

Now I understood why Lea hadn't called. She'd lost her entire shop.

"Britt, right?" I said. My voice was soft, careful. She looked tired, the skin under her eyes gone gray and raw. "Is Lea here?"

Britt shook her head. "No, she went to her mom's. I can give you the address if you want."

She scribbled on a scrap of paper, handing it over with a knowing look. My heart pounded as I turned to leave, clutching it like a lifeline—grateful Britt didn't grill me.

As I arrived at the house, the sun dipped below the horizon, casting a warm glow over the yellow-painted exterior. Lea's car was parked outside, a reassuring sign that injected me with a burst of hope. I lingered in the car for a moment, trying to organize my thoughts and come up with the right words to say.

Eventually, I abandoned the effort, trusting that it would come when I saw her. I knocked softly on the door, careful not to startle her. There was no way she'd anticipate my arrival at her mother's house—especially at night. However, my gentle knock went unnoticed.

I knocked again, a little louder. Still nothing. I waited, straining for any sound, any sign of movement from inside. The silence stretched, and a knot tightened in my gut. I wasn't leaving until she heard me.

One more knock, harder this time, and the door creaked open under my fist. I hesitated, then stepped inside.

"Lea?"

My voice echoed through the dimly lit hall. The air was thick with the scent of dust, and I moved through the house, my footfalls too loud, the silence too heavy.

I found her in the living room. She was curled up on the floor by the window, where she must have watched the sun set over the empty street. Her arms wrapped tightly around herself, and her head was buried as if hiding from the world. I heard the muffled sobs before I even saw her face, and the sound hit me like a punch to the chest.

This was what she'd been dealing with alone, the enormity of it all collapsing around her. The sight of her, so vulnerable and raw, was almost more than I could bear. I had been so consumed with my own fears that I hadn't stopped to consider that she might be drowning, that the silence was more than avoidance—that it was despair.

I dropped to my knees beside her, the sight of her, inconsolable on the threadbare rug, knocking the breath from my lungs. I didn't know what to say, how to fix it. I wanted to pull her into my lap, fold her up and tell her nothing would ever touch her again. But it was her shop, her house, her heartbreak, and I was just an intruder.

I settled down on the floor, ensuring there was an inch of space between us, and tried to find my lost voice. "Lea," I whispered gently. She flinched but remained still. "I'm here."

She turned to me, her eyes red and swollen, almost bruised-looking. For a moment, I thought she might ask me to leave. But instead, she just stared at me, hollow-eyed, as if I were another cruel illusion her mind had conjured.

I did what I've never been good at: I waited. I waited for her to come to terms with herself, to lash out at me, or to send me away. I was ready for any of it. But she only tucked her chin down, avoiding eye contact, her breath catching in slow, shuddering waves.

I sat cross-legged, my elbows on my knees, silently matching her inhale for inhale, exhale for exhale. I wanted to touch her, but I didn't. I couldn't. Not unless she asked.

Eventually, she wiped her nose on the sleeve of her sweatshirt and let her head loll back, exposing her throat and the sharp curve of her jaw. Her voice, when it came, was brittle as the bones of a starved bird. "Did Britt call you?"

I shook my head. "No. I just—I had to see you."

For a long time, she just stared at me, like she didn't quite know how to let me in. Then she shook her head, a wet hiccup of a laugh escaping her. "I haven't even started clearing out her bedroom," she said, voice scraping on the word *her*. "I left everything. The closet, her shoes... She's been gone months and I still can't even move the goddamn toothbrush from the bathroom counter. Is that pathetic or what?"

"Not pathetic," I said. "You don't let go of people like that in a weekend. Or a year. Or ever, sometimes."

She swiped at her face, half-defiant. "I thought if I just left it there, it wouldn't really be gone. But I walked through the shop today, and it was like... every piece of her life was turning to mold. And I still couldn't make myself box it up." Her voice dropped, barely audible. "I'm sorry for not calling. I just didn't know what to say. Didn't want to ruin whatever-this-is with all this... mess."

I shook my head, inching a little closer. "You could call and scream at me for an hour and it wouldn't ruin anything."

She let out a sound—almost a laugh, almost a sob—and scrubbed her hands over her face. She seemed smaller today. I realized, seeing her now, how much of her I'd missed in the last three days, and how much I wanted to un-miss, if I could.

I sat with her like that, in silence, until the light outside went blue and brittle. I didn't try to fix it, didn't try to fill the space with easy words or empty reassurances. I just stayed, and eventually, she let herself lean against me, her head heavy on my shoulder. I held her there, as if it was the most natural thing in the world, the only thing I was ever meant to do.

She was cold. It seeped through her sweatshirt and the thin cotton of my shirt. I shifted so that her whole side pressed against my ribs, my hand braced awkwardly on the carpet behind her. We watched the last light fade off the face of the house across the street, the windows going dark one by one. There was a peace in that, somehow, in watching the world close down its day.

She spoke again, her voice almost normal. "You must think I'm a basket case," she said, not looking up.

I shook my head, then realized the gesture was wasted if she wasn't watching. "I think you're grieving," I said. "That's not a crime."

"Feels like it should be." She drew a circle on the floor with the tip of her finger, and for a second I was hypnotized by the spiral. My hand moved before my brain caught up, my thumb tracing a slow, uncertain arc over her knuckles.

She stilled, watching the contact as if it were a magic trick. Then, without warning, she grabbed my hand and used it to pull herself up so we were face to face, knees touching on the cold hardwood—her eyes red but lucid, her mouth a heartbeat's width from mine.

"Lea—" I started, but she cut me off by kissing me. Not a gentle, testing kind of kiss, but something hungry, desperate, shot through with three days of unspoken fear and want. Her lips mashed mine, her hand finding the back of my neck and yanking me in, and I almost toppled forward onto her, the surprise and relief colliding in my chest and detonating. I wrapped my arms around her and held on, not caring that we were both sitting on a floor that smelled like old lemon polish and aged pine. If she needed to burn the grief out of her with a kiss, I was happy to be the torch.

We broke apart, both of us gasping, and she laughed, a ragged sound that seemed to shake some of the darkness loose.

"Sorry," she whispered, brushing her nose against mine. "I just... needed to remember what it was like to feel something good. Anything good."

"You don't have to be sorry," I said, pushing her curls off her face. "If it helps, I haven't felt good in three days. Not since you left."

Chapter Thirteen

Lea

I DIDN'T WANT COMFORT, I didn't want tenderness, I didn't want to talk about it anymore—I wanted to drown out the mess inside me with something hot and vivid and visceral. I wanted the hardness of his body pressed into mine, the kind of ache that had nothing to do with grief and everything to do with sensation. I wanted to obliterate the sadness with pleasure so intense I wouldn't be able to think, let alone remember what I had lost.

I pulled away from him and wiped my sleeve over my eyes. "Upstairs," I said, and it came out cracked and low, more a command than a request. "Now."

Rick's brow furrowed, searching my face for signs of what I really meant, but I didn't give him time to reason it out. I grabbed his hand and hauled him upright, ignoring the way my knees shook as I led him up the staircase.

At the end of the hall was my old bedroom, the same one I'd repainted pale blue when I was twelve and then cluttered with posters, plants, and the detritus of girlhood until Mom died and I couldn't stand to sleep here anymore—I'd been staying with Britt since her funeral. I shoved the door open, the air inside cool and still and threaded with dust motes. The mattress was in the middle of the floor, stripped of linens, the window half open to let in the spring night. It was bare and ugly and honest—just like I felt.

I turned, releasing Rick's hand, and stared at him for a beat, daring him to ask if I was sure. He didn't. He only stepped closer, his golden eyes soft and consuming, waiting for whatever I'd do next. I wished I could say I reached for him gently, but it was more like tearing at him: desperate hands under his shirt, fumbling with his belt, dragging him forward by the hips. He let me, his arms caging me against the wall, his mouth hot and solid on my neck, his breath filling my ears. He wanted me as much now as the first night, and thank god for that, because I needed him to devour me. It was the only way I could prove to myself I was still here.

We shed clothing without ceremony, only the rawness of people who know each other's bodies, each fault line and tremor. My hands raked over his chest, nails digging into the dusting of fur there, and he hissed through his teeth, pinning my wrists above my head and grinding his hips into mine. The length of him, already hard, pressed through denim and none of it felt polite. Just hunger and the dark, low kind of want that didn't care about pretty words or fresh bedsheets.

He kissed me with bruising force, and our bodies crashed together, knocking over the last box stacked beside the window. I ran my tongue over his shoulder, tracing the line where skin met tawny fur and muscle. He shuddered, tilting his head back, the cords of his throat thrumming under my hands. With every breath, I felt more alive.

His hands were everywhere at once—spreading me over the mattress, holding my hips, tangling in my hair. I clawed at his waistband, dragging his pants down with frantic urgency. He was huge and hot and ready and when he pressed into me, it was a shock of sensation, as if the world snapped back into color all at once. I gasped, clinging to him, and his mouth crashed onto mine with a low, rumbling sound that was half a groan, half a snarl. I didn't care if the neighbors heard.

I grabbed him by the horns—literally, wrapped both hands around the sweet curve of them—and pulled his face down to mine, kissing so savagely our teeth knocked together. He fucked me slow at first, as if afraid I might shatter, but I wrapped my legs around his hips and bit his lip until he got the message. Harder. More. I needed to disappear inside him.

He growled, the sound vibrating through his whole ribcage and into me, and I arched back, letting him take me. I wanted to be ruined by pleasure, to purge every trace of loss from my system through my fingertips, my thighs, my tongue.

He flipped me onto my stomach, hands braced at my hips, his movements purposeful and unyielding. I moaned into the pillow, gripping the mattress for balance as he drove into me, deep and ruthless, every thrust a promise that I still belonged to the world, that I could still be wanted. The bedroom spun, the entire house seemed to tilt, and I surrendered to the rhythm—the crash of our bodies, the slap of skin, the way my name sounded when he moaned it into my hair.

He bent over me, crushing his chest to my back, his hand fisting in my curls as if he could anchor me to the moment by sheer force. I reached back, clutching him, digging in with as much desperation as I felt.

He panted into my ear, "Lea, I want you. I want all of you." The edge in his voice was sharp, torn between reverence and hunger. He slammed into me, relentless, making me scream and then sob and scream again. Every thrust was a desperate plea to god or the universe or maybe just my own battered heart to let me belong somewhere, anywhere. Here. Now.

I came hard, tears and snot and sweat all mixing as pleasure yanked me inside out. I lost myself so completely in the moment that for a few seconds, everything else burned away, and I was nothing but a shriek of want and a trembling body. He felt me clench, heard the way my breath broke, and followed me over the edge, collapsing with a shudder and a final, thunderous groan that rattled the old windows and shook the dust from the ceiling. He stayed inside me as we fell, our limbs tangled, his face buried in the crook of my neck. For a while, neither of us moved. The night air cooled the sweat off our backs, and outside, city lights flickered faintly through the window. I felt the old house catch its breath around us, as if even the ghosts were stunned into silence.

He tried to kiss away the salt from my cheeks. I let him. He whispered my name again and again, softer each time, until it was just a vibration through his lips. I pressed my palms to his chest, feeling the aftershocks of his heart. There was a soreness inside me, a warmth, and for the first time in days, I didn't feel empty.

After a while, he rolled off, pulling me with him so we ended up side by side on the dead mattress. We stared at the ceiling. He traced lazy circles on my thigh.

He was the first to speak. "You know we're both a mess, right?"

"Obviously."

He snorted, his hand moving to rest heavy and comfortable across my stomach. "We could open a support group. 'Emotionally Disastrous But Smoking Hot.' Meetings every Tuesday."

"First rule is no feelings," I said, lips twitching. "Second rule is absolutely no crying. But the third is that anyone who shows up late buys the pizza."

A silence fell, but it wasn't the bad kind. More the kind that seeps in after the worst storm, when everything is debris but also—somehow—lighter. I felt the heat of him at my back, the ridiculous comfort of his arm anchoring me. It was weird how quickly I'd adjusted to needing him next to me, like my bones and muscles had been waiting for this shape to press into.

I was just beginning to drift into a haze of thoughts when Rick's voice cut through the fog. "Let me help."

"Hmm?" I turned my head slightly, raising an eyebrow in his direction. His offer could pertain to any number of things; after all, I felt like a tornado had swept through my life, leaving chaos in its wake.

"Let me help with the shop," he continued, his voice firmer, like he already knew I'd try to shut him down. "I mean it. You're not doing this alone. Not the cleanup, not the house, not any of it. I can fix things—I'm good at it. It's kind of the only thing I've ever been good at. Let me try."

I opened my mouth to protest, maybe to tell him I didn't want to be a charity case, or that he didn't owe me anything just because we were—whatever we were. But the words wouldn't stick. He was watching me with those honey-dark eyes, steady and stubborn, braced for resistance.

"Yeah," I whispered, shifting onto my back so I could see him properly. "You can help."

Rick didn't say anything, just pulled me into his arms, holding me in the safety of his embrace.

We lay in the dark, the house humming gently around us. I felt the words forming before I even knew I'd say them. "I'm going to sell it," I said, voice thin and shaky. "The house. It's just... too much. I can't do it all, not like this. I will use the money to fix up the store here and finish the Hallow's Cove shop—really be able to start fresh." I didn't know if I was saying it for him or for myself, but as soon as I said it, the choking weight in my chest loosened by a fraction.

Rick nodded, quiet and certain. "You'll make it work. I know you will. And if you need me to haul boxes, or get you an awesome deal on materials, or just... be there, I'm your man." He grinned, sheepish and a little bashful. "And if you need something demoed? Hell, I'll bring Randy and his whole crew. We'll knock it out in a day."

I turned to look at him, incredulous. "Seriously? You'd drive a crew all the way down here for this disaster?"

He shrugged, as if it was obvious. "I get a kick out of demolition. Plus, you should see the look on city contractors' faces when a bunch of ogres and lizardmen stroll in like they own the place."

I couldn't help it—I laughed, the sound strange and new in this house. "God, I'd pay to see that."

Rick's arm tightened around me, the weight of it warm and steady. "So let me do it," he said. "Let me help. Not just for you, but for your mom, too. We don't leave things half-done in Hallow's Cove. It's the code."

I pressed my face into his shoulder. "Okay," I said. "We'll do it your way. Tomorrow, we call Randy. And then we start over."

"Hell yes," Rick said, voice muffled by my hair. "We'll level the place and build it back up to something even better. Just like the one in Hallow's Cove."

His optimism was absurd, almost reckless. I found myself wanting to believe it.

After a while, when the quiet had gotten heavy again—this time with the promise of sleep, not the threat of old ghosts—Rick yawned, long and loud, then poked me gently in the side. "So."

"So?"

He shifted, propping himself on an elbow. "I'm not letting you get away with this, you know. You owe me a date."

It took me a moment to catch on, then I remembered our pact to kick things off with an actual date. The idea of acting like it was our first date, after everything we'd been through, made me chuckle.

"I usually like to go on several dates before I let someone witness me sobbing like a raccoon who lost its trash can."

He huffed, nipping at my neck. "You have to set the bar low. Otherwise I get nervous and say dumb things, and then you'll realize I'm not nearly as cool as I look."

I snorted, rolling to face him properly. "You have literal horns. You could show up in a clown suit and I'd still think you're cool."

He blinked, like he didn't quite believe me, but there was a lopsided, unguarded smile on his face I'd never seen before. It was like watching the sunrise find a window it hadn't ever touched.

"Seriously," I said, needing him to hear it. "You're more than enough, Rick. Even on your worst day."

He looked away, and for a second, I wondered if I'd pushed him too far into the open. But then he pulled me in, tucking my head under his chin, breathing me in like I was a bouquet that could only ever be beautiful, and not just a person who came with a damp house and unexpected emotional baggage. I let myself be held, let the quiet say what we couldn't. Tomorrow would bring tools and noise and mess, but for now, we just existed—awkward, wrecked, but together.

Chapter Fourteen

Lea

THE NEXT FEW DAYS were a whirlwind. True to his word, Rick called in a favor with Randy. He showed up that weekend with a crew of lizardmen, gorgons, and even what appeared to be a troll. They split up, half of them taking on the demo of the shop in town, the other half, perhaps the more careful half, started emptying out my childhood home.

I had tearfully sorted it with Rick and Britt—who had become comrades-in-arms, taking turns holding me together when I cried over a stuffed animal or a recipe box. By the time the crew came up, everything was organized by keep, donate, discard.

Britt had concocted a game plan with military precision. She'd color-coded the boxes, made a spreadsheet on her phone, and even drafted Randy's troll to do the heavy lifting. There was something both hilarious and a little bit breathtaking about watching a literal mountain of a man in a neon vest gently cradle my old lava lamp as if it were a baby bird. Rick mostly directed traffic, though every so often he'd get impatient and carry half a sofa by himself, horns nearly gouging the door frame on the way out.

The demo of the old shop was brutal but quick—like ripping off a bandage, if the bandage were forty years of shared memories and water damage. I let myself cry, but only when no one was watching. I figured I'd earned some dignity after the last week of public meltdowns. The new crew swept in, and by the end of Saturday, the shop was hollowed to its bones, every trace of my mother's handwriting and dried flower arrangements swept into the dumpsters out front. I watched the whole thing, numb but not hopeless. I tried to imagine what it would look like when it was all rebuilt, when bright paint and new fixtures erased the stink of mold and loss. I could almost see it: a clean slate, blank as a sunrise.

Britt was a lifesaver. She kept the coffee coming and the snark dialed to a gentle hum. When the last shelf came down, she handed me a beer and said, "I know you're grieving, but this is the part where you get to be a little bit excited, too."

I wanted to believe her, so I did.

After the dust settled, I did something I wasn't sure I'd ever have the nerve to do: I handed Britt the lease for the city shop. She stared at it for a long moment, then looked up at me, mouth open, like she thought it was a trick.

"You're serious?" she said, voice catching.

"Dead serious." I gave her my best attempt at a grin, even though everything inside me trembled with the risk. "I want you to have it. Or run it, at least, until you're sick of it or I'm dead."

She shook her head, then grabbed me in a bear hug so fierce I thought my ribs might pop.

"I'll take care of her," she whispered, and I realized she meant my mother, too. I let myself cry then, but only a little, and only when Britt turned away to bark orders at Randy's crew.

By Monday, the house was stripped of everything but echoes. Rick took the last few boxes to my car, his stride careful, not wanting to scuff the hardwood or my feelings. I followed him room by room, touching every wall, every window, as if my fingerprints could hold it together a little longer. When we finished, all the lights were off except for the soft glow of the porch light. I stood on the threshold, not wanting to step out and make it final.

Rick must have seen me hesitate. He set the last box in the backseat and came up behind me, arms wrapping around my waist, chin warm against my shoulder.

"You did it," he murmured, squeezing me gently. "You're really doing it."

I let myself lean back into him, just for a second. "Yeah. I guess I am."

We stood there, pressed together, watching the dark spill through every empty window. I tried to imagine someone else living here—different shoes in the entry, strange laughter echoing off the tile. Instead, I saw my mother refilling the bird feeder, or reading a trashy novel in her ratty old bathrobe. For a split second, I wanted to grab Rick and run. Hide from the future, from the ache of closing a chapter that had started before I was even born.

But I didn't.

I closed the door, locked it, and handed the keys over to the realtor on the porch without looking back. It was done. I'd cut the last tether, and now there was nothing to do but hope I wouldn't float away.

The house sold faster than I expected. A bidding war broke out within twenty-four hours. By week's end, I had a wire transfer in my name and a congratulations email with a PDF of the signed closing docs. My mother's house, her life, was officially not mine anymore. I should have felt lighter, but the grief came back in little bursts, like hiccups that refused to be soothed.

Rick headed back to Hallow's Cove, but not before forcing me to promise—pinky promise—I would return the following day. I spent one last night at Britt's, nursing an entire bottle of wine on her couch and watching true crime shows until my eyes hurt. Britt pulled a pillow over her face and groaned every time I announced a new theory about the murder, but she didn't try to fix me or talk me out of my spiral. She just listened and tossed popcorn at my head and let me be a mess, which was all I needed from her. When I finally shut the TV off, it was two in the morning and I didn't even make it to the guest bed—I passed out in a heap on the carpet, wrapped in an old afghan that smelled like every late-night sleepover from high school.

When I woke up, the world was quiet and flat. A dull headache was my only company. The closing check was still unread in my inbox, the ink on the future dry and absolute. I scrolled through my phone—there was a text from Rick, time-stamped 3:00 a.m.:

Bring coffee when you come back. And yourself. Don't make me miss you longer than necessary.

I grinned at the screen, a ridiculous, lopsided thing that felt too big for my face. For a second, it didn't matter that my life had been razed to the foundation. There was something waiting for me—a whole town, a whole world I hadn't yet ruined or outgrown.

I packed the car, thanked Britt with another rib-shattering hug, and hit the road while the sun was still an idea on the horizon. The drive out of the city was milk-smooth and quiet. I kept waiting for the wave of panic to hit, for buyer's remorse to set in and make me wish I'd clung tighter to the past, but it didn't come. Instead, every mile that rolled under my tires felt like shedding a layer of skin I didn't need anymore. I put on a playlist Britt made for me—mostly riot grrrl classics and pop-punk anthems—and let the music clear out the last of the ghosts.

Hallow's Cove reappeared on the horizon like a storybook town, all mist and green and the faint memory of woodsmoke. The main drag was as I'd left it: tidy, a little sleepy, the monster crew's pickup trucks already parked in front of both my shop and Rick's. The minute I stepped out of my car, I caught a whiff of fresh paint and a hint of sawdust, a cocktail that instantly reminded me of him. I found myself grinning like a fool as I fished the coffee carrier from my passenger seat and made my way to Rick's shop.

He was waiting for me just inside, leaning against a shelf stacked with paint cans, arms folded over his chest like he'd been there for hours. He looked tired but content, like a man who'd finished a long job and was proud of the mess he'd made. I barely got through the door before he snatched the coffee from my hand and set it on the counter. "You're early."

"Your text said not to keep you waiting," I shot back, trying for breezy but failing, because I wanted to touch him, and I was afraid if I started I wouldn't stop. He read my mind, or maybe just my body language, and closed the distance in two strides, pulling me into a hug that was all warmth and sturdy comfort.

He smelled like coffee beans and clean sweat, and the feeling of him anchoring me to the world was so good I nearly forgot how to let go. When I finally did, he looked me up and down, eyes bright. "You look better," he said, and I realized I probably did—I was rested, scrubbed raw by tears but somehow shinier for it.

"Thanks to you and your demolition goons," I replied. "Are any of them still in one piece?"

"They're at your shop," he said, with a smirk. "Randy made breakfast burritos. Even the lizardmen are eating them, which is a little disturbing if you know their digestive systems."

I made a face. "I absolutely do not want to know about their digestive systems."

He laughed, grabbed the coffees, and steered me toward the door. "Go nap, city mouse. Maybe shower, too. You smell like tears and fast food."

I rolled my eyes, but he was right: I was beyond exhausted, a collection of nerves stapled together by too little sleep.

"I'm just going to sleep till next week," I said, only half-joking.

"Nope," Rick said, steering me across the street with one hand on my lower back. "You've got a date tonight."

I stopped dead on the sidewalk, almost stumbling. "A date?"

He didn't even blink. "Yup. Seven sharp. Dress nice, or don't, but don't wear another paint-stained shirt unless you want to break the entire aesthetic of the restaurant."

My brain short-circuited. "There's an aesthetic?" I tried to picture what counted as fine dining in Hallow's Cove. "Is this one of those places with the fancy vinegar?"

He grinned but said nothing, pulling me to the door of my shop.

"Go, sleep. I'll be here to get you at seven."

Chapter Fifteen

Rick

ALL DAY I TRIPLE-CHECKED every detail, then checked it again, because the one thing I knew about Lea was that she didn't like to be fussed over. She hated anything showy, hated attention and spectacle, but somewhere along the line I'd decided she deserved at least one night where the world bent itself into something soft and easy—just for her.

I waited until sunset, then sent her a text: *Meet me at the north end of the park, past the playground*. I didn't say more.

The twilight was just starting to frost the tops of the trees when I saw her appear, hair down, a dress that was more "I want to be comfortable" than "I'm trying to seduce you," but on her it looked like a million bucks. She moved like she didn't know how pretty she was, or else she knew and had decided to mess with me about it. She stopped short when she saw what I'd built.

There, tucked behind a stand of old-growth spruce, was a table set for two: real plates, real silverware, a white tablecloth, and about a hundred mason jars filled with wildflowers and battery candlelights. I'd commandeered them from Roan and coaxed every monster kid in town into picking flowers all afternoon, bribing them with cookies and the threat of my eternal disappointment. I'd even borrowed a damn charcuterie board from the mayor, and I wasn't sure what half the cheeses on it were called, but the effect was sweet, almost magical.

Lea slowed, her steps hesitant, like she was approaching a crime scene. When she finally reached me, she looked around, mouth doing a weird little twitch—half smile, half are-you-fucking-kidding me?

"This is..." she started, then surveyed the spread again. "Are you trying to get laid, or is this an elaborate cult initiation?"

I made a show of considering. "Both are viable outcomes. But you don't have to say yes to the cult until we finish dessert."

She snorted, and the sound was a little too loud, echoing off the spruce. "Wow. I figured you'd be the type to take a gal to Killy's and call it a night."

I shrugged, feeling my cheeks go a little warm. "I wanted to show you the nicest part of Hallow's Cove. Not the bar, or the hardware store, or even the flower shop. Just..." I gestured at the clearing, the tangle of violets and clover, the little string lights I'd wrapped through the tree branches. "This."

I expected her to laugh at me, or roll her eyes, or find some clever way to puncture the spell. Instead, she just stood there, blinking at the table in the soft, twilit glow, and for a second she looked so young and hopeful that I almost had to look away. Finally, she turned to me, grinning so wide it made her whole face bright.

"You are...this is beautiful, Rick," she whispered, and when she stepped into me, it was deliberate, her arms looping around my neck.

I breathed her in—all cinnamon and lilac and the after-sun-warmth of her skin. "You hungry?" I asked, even though she'd barely looked at the food.

She nodded, but didn't let go right away. "I'm starving," she murmured, then tipped up and kissed me, gentle and grateful and a little bit wild, just like her.

When we finally broke apart, I realized I'd been holding my breath for most of it. She sat, folding her legs under the chair with a grace that was all her own, and looked at the spread like she might cry if she stared too long. For a second, I almost apologized—for the fuss, for the effort, for making her the center of something—but her eyes, shiny in the lantern glow, made me swallow the words.

We ate. We tried every cheese, even the ones that looked like they should have been illegal. She made a face at a particularly runny blue, then snuck a wedge into my mouth when I least expected it. I retaliated by stacking three different meats onto her cracker and threatening to feed it to her if she didn't try at least one. She did, bracing herself with a preemptive swig of wine, then made a show of dying dramatically, head thrown back and tongue out.

I couldn't remember the last time I'd laughed so hard, or so freely. It was easy: the world shrank to the circle of light around our table, the hush of trees, the giddy energy that came from not having to impress anyone, not even her. We talked about everything and nothing, and every time there was a lull, she'd rest her chin in her hand and look at me in a way that made my whole body tighten, like she was memorizing me for later. For keeps.

When the sun finished its downward slide, I poured the last of the wine. Lea leaned back, arms crossed under her chest, and grinned up at me. "So what happens now? You take me out into the woods and have your way with me?"

I pretended to think. "Only if you promise not to report me to the cult recruiter."

She rolled her eyes, but the edge in her smile went soft, almost hesitant. Her hand found mine under the table, fingers weaving through. For a long, buoyant moment, everything stilled—no miscommunication, no grief, just her, me, and the crickets wrapping us in velvet.

She squeezed my hand, then squinted into the dark like she could see what I was planning before I'd even stood up. "That's not it, is it?" she said. "You've got another thing up your sleeve."

"Maybe," I said, but she already looked delighted, so I pulled her out of the chair and led her along the narrow path that wound through the trees, a gravel crunch magnifying our steps. The air was thick with green and damp wood, the sky overhead going the color of blackberries at the edge.

We broke out of the spruce and into the parking lot, where my truck waited under a sagging pine.

"You're kidnapping me," Lea said, mock-serious, but she let herself be boosted into the passenger seat, skirt bunching around her thighs as she scrambled up and folded in, small and sturdy and exactly where I wanted her. The inside of the cab still smelled like sawdust and old work boots, and she took a deep breath, then shot me a sidelong grin. "So. Where are we going?"

I shook my head. "You'll see." It was only a five-minute drive, but I went slow, savoring the hush that fell between us. She tapped her fingers on the window, humming some tune that didn't match the radio at all, and every so often she'd glance over and catch me staring like a dumbass, then look away pretending she hadn't.

The road narrowed, the trees pressed in, and at the top of the ridge the world broke open. I pulled the truck off onto a gravel turnout overlooking the entire valley—Hallow's Cove below us, the river a silver ribbon in the moonlight, the whole sweep of wilderness unspooling until it hit the next mountain. The sky was a riot of stars, and the air was cool, almost crisp.

I killed the headlights, letting the darkness swallow us whole. For a second, neither of us moved—the world so quiet that the ticking of the engine cooled to a hush and you could hear the trees settle. I went around and opened the passenger door with a flourish. Lea took my hand, letting herself be helped down even though I knew she didn't need it. She looked up at the sky and gave a low, impressed whistle.

"Holy shit."

The stars were thick tonight, stitched edge to edge across the sky, brighter than any city night. A meteor streaked past, leaving a greenish scar behind that lingered for a heartbeat. She craned her neck, losing herself in the view, and for a long moment I just stood there, watching her watch the sky. She was so beautiful when she forgot to guard herself, when she let awe crack her open.

I cleared my throat, feeling a flutter of nerves once more. "I set up something special in the truck bed for you... for us." With a smile, I opened the back to reveal a cozy nest of blankets and pillows, accompanied by a thermos of hot chocolate, all ready for a perfect evening under the stars.

Lea

I could have cried, but I didn't—my reservoir was dry, and anyway, it was too good. The truck bed was lined with a ridiculous pile of plaid blankets, a battered sleeping bag, and—because he was a dork at heart—one of those overhead camping lanterns that made the whole setup glow like a little den. There were snacks, too: a paper bag of fancy cookies from the town bakery, a bag of kettle chips, and the thermos—he hadn't lied—full of homemade hot chocolate. I clambered up, wobbly in my dress, and flopped into the pile of blankets and pillows. It all smelled like pine, and dust, and him.

Rick climbed in after me, moving slow and deliberate, like he didn't want to spook me or mess up the moment. He sat with his back to the cab, legs stretched out and hooves almost hanging over the edge and waited for me to settle before he poured two mugs from the thermos. He handed me a mug and clinked his own against it, grinning with an awkward pride. I took a sip, and the heat filled my chest. The chocolate was rich and not too sweet, just the way I liked it.

The world had gone silent except for the chorus of frogs and the crackle of distant branches. Above us the sky was a cathedral, stained with stars and the thin white hush of the Milky Way. We didn't talk. For maybe the first time since I met Rick, we just sat together, shoulder to shoulder, letting the vastness of the universe do the talking for us. It reminded me of camping with my mom as a kid—how the world always felt too big, but also safe, as long as someone was beside you. I found myself leaning into Rick, not even noticing when his arm slid around my shoulders.

The warm, easy hush of the moment stretched and shimmered, until it was so taut I could feel the tension vibrating under my skin. Every time Rick shifted, the truck bed rocked, and every time his arm tightened around me, a corresponding spark jumped inside my chest. I sipped the last of my hot chocolate, not realizing until it was gone how badly I wanted my hands free.

He set his mug aside and I heard the faint click of ceramic on metal, the sound oddly loud in the hush. I felt him looking at me, but I didn't turn—I just kept watching the sky, pretending I didn't notice the way his fingers had started tracing little circles on my shoulder, or how his thigh pressed against mine with more and more certainty.

I waited for him to make the first move—half because I wanted to see how long he could hold out, and half because I liked the anticipation. The tension built, a sweet ache, until finally his hand slid up the side of my neck, thumb under my jaw, tilting my chin toward him. There was no rush to the kiss, just a gentle press of lips, slow and searching, as if he was trying to memorize the taste of me under the stars.

I melted into him, letting the pressure of his mouth draw out every last shred of resistance. My hands found his chest, splaying over the heat of his skin beneath the button-up, feeling the steady thrum of his heart. He cradled my cheek, his other arm winding around my waist, and for a long moment we did nothing but kiss—deeper, then softer, like we could breathe the night air in and out of each other.

I didn't remember lying down, but there we were, side by side in the sea of blankets, his hand gentle at my hip, his lips lingering again and again on my mouth. I'd had sex with him before—but this was different. There was no rush, no frantic need to prove we were alive or to suffocate grief with sensation. There was only his hand drifting, slow and warm, from my waist to my ribs; only the way he nuzzled into the hollow behind my ear, breathing me in like I was the first breath after drowning.

His fingers trailed under the hem of my dress, tentative, asking permission with every inch. I shivered, not from cold but from the fragile, electric certainty that he wanted me—every part, every scar, even the parts that had nothing to do with sex at all. I let my head tip back, exposing my throat, surrendering to the flutter of his mouth, the way every brush of his hand made me feel sharper, more alive.

The air was cool on my thighs when his hand slid higher, but I was already burning, every inch of exposed skin prickling where his fingers traced. He went slow, agonizingly so, thumb stroking tender crescents at the hem of my underwear, knuckles feathering the skin above my knee. When he finally—finally—let his hand slip up and over, I gasped, hips arching into the touch.

He stilled, eyes searching mine in the lantern glow. "Okay?" he whispered, voice so low it was almost lost to the night.

I nodded, too breathless for words. "Better than okay." And it was. There was no friction in this, no pain, just a hot, slow unraveling, like every nerve in my body came awake under his hands.

He kissed me again, slower this time—mouth coaxing, savoring, not just taking. My breath tangled in my throat as his fingers slid beneath the thin band of my underwear, finding me already wet and wanting. He touched me like he had all night, all weekend, all the time in the world. I moaned softly, because it was too good to hold in, and he shushed me with the sweetest kiss, his thumb circling until I was trembling against the blanket.

I reached for the buttons on his shirt, managing to fumble them open one by one. His body was solid and warm against the chill, and when I touched him, he shuddered like it was the first time. His hand never stopped moving, never stopped drawing soft, breathless sounds out of me, even when I pressed my mouth to his shoulder and bit down, needing something to hold the world together.

He tugged my underwear off slowly and left them tangled around one ankle before pulling my dress over my head. He pressed me onto my back, bracing his arms to either side of my head. The cool air hit, goosebumps chasing up my arms, but he was there, kissing each one in turn, mouth warm and reverent. He kissed my collarbones, the dip above my heart, the small scar near my ribs from when I'd fallen out of a tree at age six. It felt like each kiss was a wordless promise: I see you, I want you, I'm not going anywhere.

He took his time. There was no hurry, no need to rush toward the finish line. The night was endless, the valley below us a secret, and for once I didn't care if there were monsters or ghosts or gods watching from the dark. Let them. I had him, and he had me, not just in the way of hands and mouths and bodies, but in the slow, deliberate claiming of hearts. I wanted it to last forever. I wanted to remember this, not as the night I let go of my grief, but the night I finally decided I had a future worth wanting.

He moved over me, big and careful, the weight of his body a perfect shelter. When he finally pressed into me, it was slow, so slow, the stretch and ache of him as much comfort as pleasure. We fit together, bodies aligning in a way that made me think of matched puzzle pieces, the kind you find in the bottom of a box after searching for years. I wrapped myself around his hips and held him there, grinding up against every inch, and he groaned into my neck, the sound so needy and desperate that it almost made me cry.

He didn't fuck me—he made love to me, and I almost hated the cliché of it, but that's what it was—something slow and deliberate, something that built and built until my body was shaking, not from what he did to me but from what it meant to be chosen by him, all of him, every broken and bruised part. He ground into me with a patience that bordered on torture, pausing every so often to check my face, my breath, the whisper of my name on my lips.

Between thrusts, he kissed me everywhere—forehead, cheekbone, jaw, even the soft place behind my ear. "You're so beautiful," he said, voice thick with wonder, and it hit me harder than anything else that night. I pulled him down, mouthing the words *don't stop* against his throat, not just meaning the movement but the moment, not wanting him to let go even when my own body started to tremble and collapse.

I came soft and slow, wave after wave, clinging to his shoulders like I might go under if I let go. He held me through it, not moving, just breathing hard, sweat slicking his skin where our bodies met. When he finally came, it was with a low, stunned grunt, his face buried in the crook of my neck, hands clamped at my hips like I was the only thing that kept him tethered to the world. I felt the shudder go through him, the throb and flood of him inside me, and I was hit with this unaccountable joy—like maybe the universe hadn't made a mistake after all, putting us here, together, under this free country sky.

Afterward, we just lay there, his body draped half over mine like a living, breathing security blanket. The air cooled quickly, prickling sweat on my skin, but I didn't care. I pulled him closer, arms locked around his back, and listened to the frantic thunder of his heart gradually slow, the way his breath caught and hitched every time I stroked his hair or traced the arch of his horns. My own heart was steady, grounded, not frantic for the first time in months.

When he finally slid off me, it was gentle, almost apologetic, like he was sorry to let the night back in. He pulled my dress back over my head, then wrestled his own shirt on without buttoning it, and we lay there, side by side, sharing a half-packet of cookies and the rest of the hot chocolate. I'd never felt so completely seen, or so thoroughly wrecked.

Eventually, the night got too cold, even for us. I shivered, pulling the blankets up, and Rick sat up, stretching with a wince. "C'mon," he said, patting my knee and helping me up. "Let's get you home."

I blinked, still half-lost in the afterglow, then realized he was already hopping off the tailgate, reaching back to gather up mugs and wrappers and the little lantern. There was a note of finality in the way he moved, not cold, but—gentle. Like he wanted to wrap the night up without shattering whatever spell we'd put ourselves under.

I followed him into the cab, the warmth inside a shock after the chill outside. He started the engine, then paused, resting his hands lightly on the wheel. "That was... fuck, Lea. I don't have words for it."

My cheeks flared, and I buried my nose in my shoulder, not wanting to make it a big thing, even though it was. "Yeah," I said, and it sounded thin, so I tried again. "Me too. I don't think I ever—I mean, I never—did it like this," I finished, feeling a little embarrassed by the nakedness of the thought. "With anyone."

Rick reached over, squeezing my hand tight, his thumb tracing little nervous lines along the bones.

He didn't say anything else until we pulled up to my apartment. The street was empty, and the only sound was the click of the cooling engine. He cut the lights and turned to me, his face half-shadow in the cab.

"I had a plan for tonight," he said, voice soft but steady. "Thought I'd take you home after, like, a proper date. Walk you to your door and leave you wanting more, like a gentleman."

I grinned, a little sleepy, a little delirious from the rush of the night. "You mean you weren't going to try and seduce me in the truck bed?"

He snorted, but there was a flicker of seriousness in his eyes. "No, I wasn't. I mean, I wanted to, but that wasn't the point." He let out a slow breath, collecting his words. "I wanted to show you that you're worth more than just a quick fuck and a night on a mattress. I wanted to do it right. I wanted to... I don't know. Prove I could be the kind of guy you'd want to keep around."

He let the words hang, not looking at me, but the way his hand clenched the steering wheel gave away everything he was trying not to say.

I wanted to tell him that I'd never met anyone like him. That he was already the standard by which I would judge every other man for the rest of my life, and all of them would fall short. But I didn't know how to put that into words that weren't embarrassing or too much or, worst of all, so honest that saying them might make him disappear.

So I settled for the simplest thing: "You already did."

I leaned over the battered center console, slipped my fingers around the back of his neck, and kissed him, slow and deep and with all the certainty I didn't know I had until it was unlocked by his stubborn, messy, beautiful devotion. When I pulled away, he was grinning, a little dazed, like he'd just discovered a new law of physics.

He squeezed my thigh, just above the knee, and let the silence fill up between us until it felt as peaceful as the cold night beyond the windshield. I wanted to stay there, soaking up the warmth and the hush and the way he looked at me like we were the only two creatures on Earth. But there was a point, with every good night, where you had to open your door and trust the world would still be waiting in the morning.

I slid out of the truck, shivering as my feet hit the cold earth. He followed, not giving me a chance to protest, to the door, hand warm at the small of my back the whole way. At the threshold, neither of us moved.

He reached up, tucked a strand of hair behind my ear, and said, "Text me when you wake up?" Like it wasn't a given, like it was the most fragile hope in the world.

I found his hand and squeezed it. "I will." After everything, it seemed stupid and impossible to want more, to trust that wanting more wouldn't ruin all the good built up in the last few hours. But the words didn't scare me this time. I wanted to text him. I wanted to tell him everything.

He kissed my forehead, a quick, almost embarrassed brush, then stepped back and walked to the truck. He waited at the curb until he saw my lights come on inside.

I leaned my head against the door after it closed, listening to the slow beat of my own heart, the way the walls echoed back the contentment I'd managed to borrow from the stars. Hours later, wrapped in my own blankets, I lay awake and replayed every second of the night again and again, like a favorite song. There was a new ache inside me, but it wasn't loneliness—not exactly. It was the kind of ache you get when something you never thought you'd have was suddenly, miraculously, yours.

Chapter Sixteen

Rick

With Lea back in Hallow's Cove, her city life wrapped up and squared away, we fell into a rhythm. We traded off nights at each other's apartments. I worked at my shop during the day, but snuck away at odd hours to help her with hers.

At first, there was nothing much to do but wait. Every morning I'd walk over and find her cross-legged on the floor, staring at paint swatches or hunched over a laptop, drafting up to-do lists that bordered on the metaphysical: Fix the floor. Replace the windows. Make Mom proud. Start over. Some days I'd find her with her hands deep in potting soil, sleeves rolled to her elbows, a streak of dirt on her forehead like a war stripe. She'd be talking to her seedlings as if they were old friends. I kept my jokes to a minimum, because it seemed less like she was talking to herself than holding court with a thousand tiny, green confidants.

Given the progress that had already been made, Randy's crew finished the big stuff in two days. After the demo, the shop looked like one of those time-lapse videos where a building crumbles to the studs and then, impossibly, emerges shinier and more itself than before. The new floor gleamed, the windows sparkled, and the back room was dry as a bone. I handled the grit work—patching drywall, running new conduit, swapping out some ancient fuse box for the kind that wouldn't burn the whole block down after a power surge. Evenings, we'd go over the day's progress, splitting takeout or leftovers, always ending up on the floor or the work table, limbs tangled and mouths hungry. Sometimes, Lea would fall asleep mid-sentence—head on my chest, hand curled in my shirt—and I just let her, because it felt like a privilege to be the last thing she trusted before she let go.

It was the third week after coming back from the city when she started getting squirrelly. The opening was creeping closer, and her lists multiplied. She'd read one, then scribble three more things to do. She double-checked everything I touched, though I didn't mind. If it calmed her, I'd let her measure each paint stripe and count every petal on the fake sample bouquets. She was, technically, my boss for all work performed within her domain, and I liked the way she'd start to order me around, then forget what she was ordering and just stare at me until I kissed her out of her spiral.

She never said it out loud, but I could feel her nerves ratchet up a notch every day. I wanted to fix it, be the guy who made the world easier for her, but I also knew that nothing would calm her down except the thing itself: the launch, the proof that she could survive a night with all eyes on her and not collapse into a heap.

So I decided to make the opening a little easier. I fired off a text to Maisie—*Urgent, need your help, bookstore?*—and left Bryce with the hardware. By the time I crossed the street, the rain had started, drumming a steady beat on the awnings as I ducked through the door of the bookstore.

Barnaby was at the counter, nose deep in some leather-bound volume that looked older than the town itself. With the stormy light outside illuminating his pale, angular profile, he looked like he belonged in an oil painting.

"She's in the back," he said, not looking up, but his mouth curling into a hint of a smile. "Try not to break anything."

I snorted and wove my way through the shelves. I still got lost in here sometimes—Barnaby's arrangement of books was vast and varied. I found Maisie hunkered over her computer in the back room.

She didn't look up as I walked in, just kept typing with the kind of terrifying efficiency that always made me think she was secretly running the government. I hovered in the doorway until she finally glanced up, eyebrows arched, face already halfway to a smirk.

"I thought you'd come crawling back sooner," she said, pushing her glasses up on her nose. "What's the emergency?"

I closed the door behind me, shedding a little of my pride. "I need a favor."

"Is it about Lea?"

"Yeah, but not in the way you think." I sat opposite her, the scent of old paper and coffee grounds instantly calming my nerves. "She's almost ready to open the shop, but I want it perfect. Grand opening, big community thing. I want her to feel like this place is hers, that she belongs."

Maisie's eyes lit up, equal parts vampiric mischief and genuine warmth. "You want the full Hallow's Cove welcome committee," she said. "Don't play coy, Rick—I've seen you decorate for Halloween. You're a sucker for a surprise party."

My ears burned, but I didn't deny it. "Lea's never had anyone really root for her, Maisie. Not since her mom. I want the whole town here."

Maisie spun in her chair, already opening her calendar. "What's the timeline?"

"Friday night. Seven p.m. She wants to soft open then, but I want it to be... big."

Maisie whistled low. "Short notice. Lucky for you, my organizational prowess is legendary. I'll get the flyers up at Killy's and Cool Beans. Mitch and Clay can do pastries and coffee. Roan will design the signs."

I exhaled, a little more relaxed. "What about Barnaby?"

"You know he'll close early. He secretly loves that stuff." She arched a brow and leaned forward. "So what's the rest of the plan, hotshot? Gonna sweep her off her feet, or just give a toast and call it good?"

My jaw flexed. "I want her to know she's not alone. I want her to see—really, actually see—how much people care. If I'm all in, I want to show her she's not just...tolerated here. She's wanted."

Maisie smiled like she saw through me, down to the bare beams. "You know, for a guy with horns, you wear your heart right out in the open."

"Does it make me a sap?"

"Maybe. But you picked the right vampire to help. I'll make it rain humans and monsters, Rick. Leave the rest to me."

I stood up, feeling lighter—like letting someone else take a little of the load made space for something new to grow. "Thanks, Maisie."

I left with a spring in my step, the rain pelting my face on the way out, cold but invigorating. If I hurried, I could finish the wiring in Lea's shop before she noticed her fancy new sign was already delivered. For once, I wanted to beat her to the punch.

It was almost dusk when I circled back to the shop. The lights inside glowed warm and promising, illuminating the mess of cardboard and bubble wrap that signaled we were almost ready. Lea was hunched over her laptop at the front counter, her hair tied up in a paint-splattered scarf, concentration furrowing her brow. She didn't hear me at first, so I just watched—stealing a minute to memorize her, the way she chewed on the end of her pencil and muttered softly at the screen. It stunned me how much she already belonged here, even before the sign had even gone up.

I leaned in the doorway, admiring, and when she finally looked up, her expression changed from fierce focus to soft and goofy in a heartbeat. "Hey," she said, like it had been minutes, not hours, since we'd last crossed paths.

I nodded toward the counter. "You lost in Excel hell again?"

She groaned theatrically, rolling her eyes. "I swear these invoices breed at night. You'd think I was trying to solve world hunger, not order biodegradable seed pots."

I crossed the room, smirking, and plucked the laptop from under her fingers. "Let me rescue you."

Lea tried to snatch it back, but I held it up out of reach. Even on tiptoe, she was a good foot below my chin, which only made her scowl more dangerous. "Rick, if you delete my spreadsheets, I'll murder you and use your horns as plant stakes."

I gave her a kiss on the cheek and handed it over, arms raised in submission. "Wouldn't dream of it, flower girl. But you've got to let me take you home. You look like you're two more line items away from a nervous breakdown."

She laughed, cheeks flushed, and leaned against my chest as I folded her in for a hug. I could feel the tension in her back, all wound up and quivering like an overtuned guitar string.

"I want to get this right," she murmured into my shirt, voice small and tired.

"You will," I said, steady and certain.

She allowed me to escort her to her apartment above the shop, her bags and laptop casually draped over one shoulder.

"Can we get takeout?" Lea asked, leaning against me. "I need a quiet night in."

"Mmm, what are you thinking?" I pushed the door open and ushered her to one of the few chairs.

"How about Thai?"

When the food arrived, we sprawled on the couch, cartons between us, and played a stupid movie in the background. She ate with one leg slung over mine, scooping noodles with effortless dexterity, and when she dripped sauce on the couch, she just wiped it with her wrist and kept talking. I loved her for all the little human things, the imperfections she refused to hide.

After, she curled into my side like she always did and closed her eyes, fingers tracing circles on my thigh. "You know what I wish?" she murmured, half-asleep.

"What's that?"

"I wish tomorrow was already opening night. So I could walk in and just...be done worrying." Her voice was velvet soft, full of longing and exhaustion.

I kissed her forehead. "It's going to be perfect, Lea. You know that, right?"

She hummed, unconvinced but comforted, and nestled closer. "Maybe. I'll believe it when I see people in there. When I see someone pick up a bouquet and smile and it isn't just you pretending."

"Hey, I'm a damn good actor," I protested, grinning. "You should see me with a bunch of tulips. I get weepy."

"Liar," she said, though I could hear the smile in her tired voice.

I kissed her again, slow and sleepy, and we drifted together until the late evening light faded out and the only thing left was the easy hush of her breathing in my arms.

Chapter Seventeen

Lea

FRIDAY CAME FAST. I barely slept the night before, waking up every hour to mentally list all the things I still had to finish. The morning started with a downpour, so loud against the shop roof that it felt like a warning shot. I brewed coffee strong enough to make my hands shake, then spent the whole day pacing up and down the shop, triple-checking each shelf, plant, and price tag. Rick, meanwhile, was a blur of motion—hanging signs, polishing windows, even running out to pick up a flat of last-minute annuals when I realized I'd forgotten to order any poppies. He never stopped moving except to squeeze my shoulder or quickly kiss my cheek.

By 4:00 p.m., the rain had stopped and the clouds had drained out to sea, leaving the whole cove washed clean and bright. I was still wearing my ratty paint jeans and a T-shirt splattered with at least three different shades of green when Rick came jogging in from the backyard, cheeks flushed with wind and triumph.

"Hey!" he barked, startling me out of my inventory trance. "It's time. Get going."

"Going where?" I asked, half-distracted by the miniature cacti I was alphabetizing.

He grinned, wide and wolfish. "Home. Shower. Hair. Change. You're not hosting your grand opening looking like an extra from a seed catalog."

I opened my mouth to argue, but he cut me off with a gentle but unyielding hand on my lower back, steering me toward the door.

"I mean it, Lea. Go get ready. I'll finish up here and meet you back at the apartment."

I let myself be herded, a little dazed by his energy. My feet squelched in my battered sneakers as I tromped upstairs, shedding layers of grimy clothes with every step. The apartment was its usual disaster, but the bathroom was a little island of calm: clean towels, a new candle (cinnamon vanilla), and two toothbrushes in the cup instead of one. My chest went weirdly tight at the sight.

Before I could overthink it, I jumped in the shower and scoured away three days of sweat, paint, and dirt. I even shaved my legs—first time all week. I took extra time co-washing my hair, silently thanking Rick for giving me enough time to care for my curls. Then I tore through drawers and found one of the summer dresses I'd packed for "special occasions," which I hadn't worn since that first night at Killy's. I removed my hair from one of

Rick's soft shirts I wrapped it up in, working through product and styling my curls. I caught my reflection in the ancient, paint-speckled mirror. I looked... not put together, not beautiful, but alive. Electric, almost. Like something was burning inside me and leaking out my eyes and cheeks.

I was still barefoot and brushing my teeth when Rick banged through the door, arms full of flower bundles and a bag from Cool Beans I suspected was filled with pastries and not, as advertised, "emergency supplies." He stopped short when he saw me, something raw and unguarded moving across his face.

"You clean up nice," he said, voice low and almost reverent.

"You see me every morning like a swamp creature," I shot back, feeling self-conscious but also—strangely—wanting him to see all of it, every version of me.

He shrugged, setting the armful of flowers down on my counter and coming closer. He ran his thumb around my jaw, not bothering to hide the way he lingered on the spot near my ear where my hair still dripped onto my neck.

"I like the swamp creature. But this?" He let out a slow whistle that made me squirm. "This is unfair. You're gonna kill 'em out there."

I rolled my eyes but smiled, turning away so I didn't start giggling like a teenager. "Are you here to make me nervous, or are you here for something else?"

"Both?" He plopped onto the edge of the bed, grinning. "Mostly, I came to steal five minutes of your time before you go and charm the socks off the whole town."

I turned to face him, hands fidgeting with the cord of my dress. "Five minutes?"

He crooked his finger, summoning me. When I stood in front of him, he slid his hands up my thighs, fingers splayed possessively. "Nervous?"

"I'm terrified," I admitted, swallowing.

His grin faded, replaced with that deep steadiness I'd come to crave. "You've done things that are so much harder than this, Lea. You already built it. All this is just letting them in."

I tried to hold onto that, the warmth of his words. "Still want them to like me, though. Is that pathetic?"

"I'd be more worried if you didn't." He drew me closer until my knees touched his. "As long as you remember that I already do." He leaned in, kissing just below my jaw, then lower, over the flutter of my heart.

God. He was completely unfair. "You're going to make me smudge my mascara," I warned, even as I wound my fingers through his hair and let myself collapse into the kiss. He tasted like everything I'd ever wanted, ever been brave enough to wish for. I wanted to stay tangled with him forever, but after a minute I broke away, breathless.

"Is there a time limit on those five minutes?" I asked.

He grinned, teeth flashing. "There's always time for you."

One more kiss, quick and hungry, and he nudged me toward the door. "Go," he said softly, "before I wreck all your hard work getting pretty."

I gathered my bag, found a clean pair of sandals, and we walked down together, out into the scented dusk. Rick squeezed my hand, steady and grounding.

The windows of Coming Up Daisies were all aglow. I could see Maisie through the front glass, already there with a camera, fussing with the decorations. Inside, the shop was transformed: every shelf and table teeming with color and light, the air sweet with blossom and sugar and the musk of freshly cut stems. There were more people here than I'd seen in one place since moving to Hallow's Cove. Some from Rick's circle, some from the coffee shop, a few faces from Killy's, and—my heart stuttered—Barnaby, rising like a specter among the arrangements, elegant in a tailored deep blue suit. He caught my eye the moment I entered, inclined his head once, and offered the smallest, most gracious of smiles, as if I'd passed some secret test.

I was ushered to the register by Roan, who'd made a brilliant new logo and insisted I pose for a Polaroid before she'd let anyone else buy so much as a single marigold. Behind the counter, they'd strung up a banner; it had "Opening Day!" in wild, painted letters, where every word bloomed with hand-drawn vines and tiny, grinning sunflowers. The whole place looked alive, humming with possibility. It was exactly what I'd dreamed but never dared to ask for.

Within minutes, the bell above the door was ringing, letting in a steady current of customers—neighbors, regulars from the coffee shop, even a group of awkward high schoolers who immediately started cracking jokes about "carnivorous plants" and pretending to feed each other's sweaters to the Venus flytraps. It should have been overwhelming, but I found myself beaming, laughing, fluttering from the register to the displays and back again, answering questions about soil and light, snipping ribbons, making up impromptu bouquets on the fly. Every interaction left me a little more dizzy, a little more convinced that maybe, just maybe, I could make it work here.

When the rush hit its peak, Rick hovered near the back wall, more bouncer than boyfriend, arms folded and keeping a watchful eye over the proceedings. His smile was proud, indulgent, and a little awed—like he couldn't quite believe I belonged to him. I caught him staring a few times and stuck my tongue out in retaliation. The tips of his ears went pink, which was all the reward I needed.

The evening blurred in a riot of color and conversation. I lost track of how many times people congratulated me, how many hands I shook, how many times I had to dodge an overly eager hug from a customer. I felt like a country fair prize pig—admired, petted, slightly overwhelmed—but instead of making me retreat, it made me want to work even harder, to give them all something extraordinary to come back for.

I caught little flashes of my new community in the crowd: Maisie, snapping pictures; Mitch, the wolfman from Cool Beans, laughing with his partner Clay and a burly rock troll over a potted rosemary; Roan, as promised, affixing her gorgeous signage to every flat surface while also somehow managing to hand out cookies on a tray shaped like a watering can. I even spotted Gwen from Killy's, crisply dressed and holding a bouquet like it was both a shield and a badge of honor. Every time I tried to thank one of them for coming, the words came out all tumbled and breathless, a little too much like the beginnings of a happy cry.

I was so distracted by the whirling, joyous chaos that I didn't notice Rick slipping out the back, but a few minutes later he returned, two champagne bottles dangling from his monstrous fingers. He made a show of popping both at once, the corks ricocheting off the ceiling while the crowd whooped and applauded like we'd hosted fireworks instead of a flower sale.

He poured me the first glass, leaning over the register to hand it to me with a soft, conspiratorial wink. "To the Queen of Daisies," he toasted, voice low enough that only I could hear. "And to her new kingdom."

I laughed, my cheeks feeling hot. "You are so dumb," I said, but when I looked at him, the moment shimmered with gratitude. Not for the toast or even the party, but for the world he'd built around me, scaffolding out of faith and bone. "But thank you," I whispered, lifting my glass to clink his. "For all of it."

He tipped his head, letting that golden grin blaze for me alone, and in that second I knew I was completely, irrevocably his.

The crowd thinned as the evening waned, the last stragglers leaving with arms full of hydrangea and cinnamon buns. I started collecting discarded cups and napkins, still half-afraid the mess would eclipse the glow of a night I didn't want to ever end. But Rick was already sweeping behind me, making short work of the debris. At one point I caught him dipping the broom handle low and spinning it like a dance partner, grinning when he saw me watching. He crossed to where I stood, took my hand with exaggerated gallantry, and pressed a kiss to the back of my fingers. "Permission to escort you upstairs, Ms. Thompson?"

I should've played coy, but I couldn't muster it. I only nodded, my heart too full to risk words. He locked the door behind us and pulled me close as we climbed the stairs, his hand gentle but insistent on the small of my back. The adrenaline of the night lingered in my veins, making every brush of contact electric. Up in my tiny apartment, the shadows felt less like a hiding place and more like a cocoon as he folded me into his arms and lifted me clear off the ground.

"You did it," Rick whispered in the hush, his voice a gentle vibration against my scalp. "You're one of us now."

I let out a shaky laugh, equal parts relief and disbelief. Tears prickled at the corners of my eyes, and I buried my face in his chest so he wouldn't see. He set me down, but I couldn't seem to let go. The world felt so big, so loud; maybe I'd built a new home here, but damn if it didn't still scare me sometimes, the size of what I'd allowed myself to want.

He hugged me tighter, reading my mind in that uncanny way he had. "You deserve this," he murmured, rubbing circles over my back with his palm. "You always did. You just needed a little proof."

He pulled back just enough to tilt my chin up, eyes molten gold in the thin light. He kissed me slow at first, deliberate, as if he was memorizing the shape of my lips, the taste of the words I hadn't said yet. Each pass of his mouth made me ache, made me want and want until I was dizzy with it.

"I want to be inside you," he said, voice a low rumble that vibrated through my bones, "before you even think about taking off that pretty dress."

I barely managed a nod before his hands swept over my hips, hauling me flush against him. The skirt bunched up, fabric cool against my thighs, his hands hot and possessive underneath it. He backed me against the wall, never breaking the kiss, and in one deft motion slid my underwear down, past my knees, past my ankles, discarding them on the floor. The shock of bare skin met cool air and the searing heat of his hands, everywhere at once, cut through me.

One thick hand lifted me by the thigh, bracing me in place, while the other undid his pants with practiced ease. I felt the heat of him, already hard, pressed against the wet, desperate ache between my legs. He slid in slow—so slow—until I was full and stretching around him, breath knocked from my lungs by the sheer size of it, the delicious fullness. I arched back, head pressing into the wall, and he kissed down my throat, right where my pulse thundered.

The world spiraled with every thrust. He fucked me, steady and deep, each movement a sweet relief after the giddy, anxious tension of the evening. I wrapped both arms around his neck, held on as he rocked into me, the muscles in his back shifting under my palms like tectonic plates. He grunted with every snap of his hips, the sound primal and hungry, and I moaned into his shoulder, half-laughing at how greedy we were, how we could never get enough.

He made me come so forcefully against the wall that I bit down on his shoulder, hard, and the only thing that saved me from sliding to the floor was his solid hold. I came back to earth straddling his hips, his cock deep inside, our breaths mingled in the hush of the dark. He thrust a few more times, rougher now, chasing the edge, and with a low, helpless growl, he came, his heat flooding me as he spilled into a gutted, quiet stillness.

We let gravity have us then, collapsing to the floor in a tangled heap, my legs still locked around his waist.

"You're going to be the death of me," he said into my hair, voice so soft I barely heard it.

"Unlikely," I whispered. "You're built much too sturdy."

"That's not what I meant." He cupped my cheek, thumb tracing the arch of my cheekbone. "You made this place come alive, you know?"

He was ridiculous, and maybe I was too, but it was suddenly so goddamn important to say it back—to name it out loud for once instead of letting it ricochet inside my chest. "You're the reason I was brave enough to try," I said, voice breaking in the middle. "I almost didn't open today. Wasn't sure I could face it. But you... you made it safe to want."

He kissed me like that was the only answer he needed. The floor was cold and the night was colder, but we didn't move. We just breathed together, letting the world shrink down to the four hands and two hearts and one breathless giggle that seemed to echo in the darkness. When Rick finally stood up, still holding me as if he could anchor me to the planet, he swept us both to the bed and tangled us under the covers like it was perfectly reasonable to never let go.

That was the first night Hallow's Cove felt like home.

Chapter Eighteen

Lea

THE MORNING AFTER THE grand opening, I woke up in a haze of sex and serotonin and the faint, cloying scent of peonies. Rick was already gone—probably wrestling with a shipment of, I don't know, self-driving wheelbarrows or whatever new hotness the hardware store was peddling—but he'd left a tray on the nightstand with coffee, a cinnamon scone, and a handwritten note: *Flowers didn't need watering. Didn't want to wake you. Miss you anyway. – Rick.* He'd dotted the "i" in his name with a little heart. The minotaur was a menace.

I lay there for a long time, staring at the ceiling, letting the new shape of my life settle into place. The hum of the shop below, the soft clatter of someone (Dixie, a brownie and my first hired help, probably) restocking the cooler, the distant whine of a leaf blower outside—the ordinary was extraordinary now. All the years I'd spent trying to keep the world at bay, all the ways I'd curled up inside myself to avoid more loss—suddenly they seemed small, almost laughable, compared to this: a town that had taken me in, a man who insisted on loving me even when I was a handful, a store that wasn't haunted by ghosts, but buoyed by them.

I got up, slipped on Rick's flannel from the chair, pulled on some leggings, and shuffled down the stairs barefoot. The air in Coming Up Daisies was damp with the last dregs of morning fog, all the colors of the petals and leaves so saturated they looked fake. Dixie was indeed at the cooler, hair tucked under a bandana, head bent over a bouquet of orange lilies and purple something-or-others.

She looked up, saw me, and grinned like the sun. "Hey, boss. You missed the post-opening donut orgy. I think Randy left you a half-eaten bear claw."

"Perfect fuel for the day," I said, and made a beeline for the counter. The bear claw was, in fact, more like a bear pinky, but I gnawed on it anyway, licking powdered sugar off my fingers like it was the price of admission for a day in paradise.

Dixie surveyed me over the top of her bouquet. "So. Wild night?"

I tried to look scandalized, but failed. "I plead the Fifth."

She snorted, setting the bouquet into a vase with a thunk. "You know, if you're going to have a whirlwind romance with the town's most eligible bachelor, you need to get used to the gossip mill. Three people already stopped by to check if you and Rick eloped after closing last night."

I paused mid-sugar lick. "Tell me you're kidding."

She made a face. "Wish I was. This is a small town, boss. The only thing people love more than fresh flowers is a good love story and you're giving 'em both." Dixie turned back to her work, humming something that sounded suspiciously like "Here Comes the Bride." I rolled my eyes, but I didn't hate it—not really. The shop was full of customers by midmorning, the bell over the door ringing every three minutes, Dixie's voice chirping greetings and snappy banter while I floated from table to table, answering questions and making tiny last-second edits to every bouquet about to walk out the door. I caught a glimpse in the front window and almost didn't recognize myself: curls natural and haloed by sun, cheeks pink, mouth stuck in a permanent lopsided smile.

A little after noon, Britt showed up—a complete surprise. She breezed in looking like she'd run a marathon through an art supply store—paint on her elbows, new nose ring, and a T-shirt that said "Feral and Thriving" in neon pink letters. She dropped a takeout bag on the counter and surveyed the shop like a general reviewing her troops, then gave me a hug tight enough to nearly pop my ribs. "I brought lunch," she announced, opening the bag with a flourish.

I grinned and dug into the bag. "Please tell me this is the greasy gyro I dream about."

"Unless you object to extra tzatziki. I also swiped baklava." She leaned in, voice sly. "So how's the new life treating you? You ready to admit I was right about you being a country girl at heart?"

I considered this, chewing. "I'm not sure I'm ready to go full Carhartt, but I do like it when people wave to me on the street."

Britt waggled her brows. "That's how it starts. Next thing, you'll be in overalls with a bandana, shooting whiskey with the old-timers at the local bar. I give it six months."

I snorted. "Not happening. I'll stick to snake bites and sarcasm, thanks."

Britt stayed until I closed up. It only took her ten minutes to step in and work side by side with Dixie. She wasn't the type to sit idly and watch someone work. She washed her hands and pulled me into a hug after the last customer left.

"You did good, Lea. Your mom would be proud." She didn't say it as a throwaway, either. She meant it, and the words landed in my chest and cracked something open that had been hardening over since the funeral. I blinked fast, then nodded and squeezed her hand.

"You sticking around?" I asked, not daring to hope.

She wrinkled her nose. "I gotta get back tonight—turns out running a flower shop in the big city is a full-time gig." She shouldered her tote. "Don't let Hallow's Cove break your heart, okay?"

"It's more likely to drown me in cinnamon rolls and small-town festivals," I said.

She laughed, and for a moment it was like we were back in college, right before the world got heavy. "That's what I'm afraid of. Call me if you need anything. Seriously, Lea. It's not weakness to need help, okay?"

She left me with a wave and a promise to visit soon, the bell over the door chiming a warm farewell. I watched her cross the street and felt a bittersweet pang in my chest.

I was cleaning up the last of the day's detritus—a pile of rubber bands, some wilted stems, a few stubborn receipts stuck to the counter—when Rick came in. He was vibrating with excitement.

"There she is," he said, sweeping me up in a hug that nearly knocked the wind out of me. "You survived your first twenty-four hours as a shop owner." He set me down, grinning so wide it looked like it hurt. "And you didn't even have to run off with a biker gang or join a snake cult to do it."

I crossed my arms. "It's early yet. Could still happen."

"Not if I get to you first," he said, and dove for a kiss that was all teeth and sunshine and barely contained pride. He plopped the cardboard box on the counter between us. "Open it."

I eyed the label: "From the collection of Barnaby and Maisie Hallow." I could tell it was Maisie's handwriting, equal parts elegant and threatening. I opened the box, and inside was...a single, battered Polaroid, a first edition of a book on heirloom gardening, and a note scrawled on thick paper.

Lea: For the record, this is us rooting for you. Keep growing (and don't kill the peonies). —M & B

Under the note, tucked between the pages of the gardening book, was a delicate pressed violet, its color still impossibly vivid. I turned the Polaroid over; it was a photo from last night, me and Rick behind the counter, arms thrown around each other, confetti from one of Roan's poppers still stuck in my hair. I was laughing with my whole face, and he was looking at me with a kind of reckless joy I'd never seen caught on film. My throat went thick.

Rick read over my shoulder, getting uncharacteristically quiet. "Y'know, I think they're right," he said, looping his arms around my waist and resting his chin on my shoulder. "You're kinda stuck with us now. Whole town's got their eye on you."

"Is that supposed to be reassuring?" I leaned into him, letting my head tip back. "Because the pressure's on. I already started planning my dramatic escape."

He kissed the top of my head. "There's nowhere you could go that I wouldn't follow, Azalea Thompson."

I almost made a joke—almost, but didn't. Instead, I reached behind me, laced my fingers with his, and just stood there for a minute, letting the moment grow roots. It didn't matter that the future was a mystery or that the only guarantee in life was more change; if I could stand here, in this tiny shop with my arms full of flowers and a man who smelled like sawdust and sunlight, I'd figure it out. I always had.

Rick

"How about you come up to my place and we order some food?" I said, attempting to sound casual but probably sounding more like a nervous game show host.

Lea squinted at me like she was trying to read the fine print on a suspicious contract. "You're plotting something."

"Am I?" I tried to pull off the innocent look, but it came out more like I was choking on a peanut.

I'd been planning this since we came back from the city, but now, standing with her in the empty shop, I could feel my nerves fizzing under my skin. I wanted her to move in. Not just sleep over, not just leave a toothbrush and an old band tee in my dresser, but to actually share a life, a roof, a calendar stuffed with grocery lists and overdue library books. I wanted her to know she was as permanent as the nails in my floorboards, as the foundation that kept the rain and wind from tearing my world apart.

But how do you sell the woman you love on the idea of waking up to your bad breath and chronic snoring every single day?

I led her out her shop door, hand in hand, the late afternoon sun painting us orange and gold. She kept up a running commentary about the day's sales, the weirdest customer requests ("Did you know someone tried to buy a bouquet for their lizard?" "For the *lizard*? Or for the lizard's birthday party?" "Unclear, but there was a cake involved, and the lizard wore a hat"). I only half-listened, because I was trying to build up the courage to say what I'd rehearsed a dozen times.

We walked through my shop and climbed the steps to my place. I unlocked the door and let her in first, resisting the urge to yell "SURPRISE!" even though there was nothing to surprise her with yet.

She flopped onto my sofa, stretching, then propped her feet up on the coffee table. "What's the game plan, captain?"

I busied myself with the takeout menus stacked on the kitchen counter. I had no idea what I was doing. "Uh, pizza? Thai? Tacos?"

"You're the worst at decisions," she said, affection in her voice. "Let me take a look." She rifled through the pile, found a battered sushi menu, and tossed it at me. "Order your favorite. I'll eat whatever. You know that."

I watched her from the kitchen, the way her whole body loosened at the end of a long day—shoulders unknotting, toes fanning out, face losing the last of its retail-welcome mask. It was the most beautiful thing I'd ever seen, and I wanted it every day. Or, at least, as many days as she'd let me have.

I put in the order—two sushi rolls, miso soup, and a surprise dessert because I liked the way her eyes lit up at the unexpected. I paced the kitchen as it processed, running through the speech in my head, then immediately discarding it because it sounded like something out of a bad rom-com.

She called out from the living room. "Hey, Rick? Why is there a new pillow on the couch that says 'Welcome Home'?"

I froze, chopsticks in one hand, phone in the other. "Uh. That's, uh. New marketing initiative. Cozy Up With Rick's Hardware."

She leaned around the doorframe, eyebrow cocked. "It has daisies on it."

Heat crept up my neck. "Yeah, you know, brand synergy."

She padded over in bare feet, pillow under one arm, and plopped down at the table where I'd already put out mismatched plates and a six-pack of local cider.

"You're hiding something." She poked my chest, hard. "Spill."

I took a deep, bracing breath. "What if I said I wanted you to move in with me?" I blurted, the words tumbling out before I could sand off the rough edges.

She blinked, mouth forming a perfect O, then squinted at me like I'd just suggested we adopt a baby capybara and raise it on bug spray and old pizza crusts.

"Move in?" she repeated. "Like... move in together, *together*?"

"Yeah," I said, and a whole platoon of nerves ignited. "Like, officially. Not just your underwear in my drawer, but your name on the deed, your shampoo in the shower, your takeout preferences permanently logged in my phone."

She blinked, then started to laugh, a hiccupy, incredulous cackle that doubled her over the table. "Wow. Is this your premeditated murder-suicide plan, or are you just really into communal bills?"

I faked offense, but only just. She held up a hand to pause me, catching her breath.

"Okay, okay, I need a minute to process this." She wandered to the window, looking out over the roofline of Main Street like she was hoping for a sign—maybe a rainbow, maybe a flaming comet. "If I move in," she said, not turning around, "do I get half the closet, or is this one of those 'all your stuff goes in the garage' situations?"

"Full half," I said. "Even the shelves. I'll clear out the power tools."

She turned then, eyes bright and wide, mouth quirked in that sly way that always made my knees go a little weak. "But what if," she said, stepping close enough to bump my hip with hers, "instead of me moving in, we knock down the wall between our places and just... make one giant space?"

I blinked. "You want to demo the wall?"

She grinned, delight radiating off her like summer heat. "Think about it. Why not? We could make a monster-sized kitchen, or a studio, or—hell, even a greenhouse if we get ambitious and Randy owes you another favor."

It was so her, to meet a proposal with a contrarian, impossible escalation. And it was so us, that my first response wasn't to say no, but to start immediately scheming how we could do it. What load bearings we'd need, how to reroute the wiring, whether we could keep the original crown molding if we just reinforced the span with a steel beam. I let the idea bloom in my head, and within seconds I was already invested.

"I know a guy," I said, voice deadpan.

She giggled, and I realized that was exactly what I'd wanted—not just for her to say yes, but for her to say yes in her own way, to meet my crazy with her own. We grinned at each other, two idiots in love, and I reached for her hand across the table.

"Deal," I said. "Let's build a life we can't escape from."

"Even if it kills us," she replied, squeezing my fingers.

"Especially if it kills us," I said, and she laughed again, pure and unfiltered.

We ate our sushi on the couch, then fell asleep watching a documentary about beekeeping.

Epilogue

Lea

I WOKE UP TO the strange sensation of moving through the world without my own permission. The room was dark, the air cool, and I was floating—no, carried—cradled against a chest that thudded steady as a drum. My arms dangled at odd angles, my cheek pressed to something warm and flannel. I squinted, disoriented, at the blur of ceiling and doorframes gliding past, then finally zeroed in on Rick's voice, soft and low as a radio turned down for the night.

"You good?" he murmured, shifting me higher in his arms as he shouldered open the bedroom door with his back. I realized then that I was being princess-carried, like a swoony heroine in a romance novel, except I was drooling a little and my legs were a deadweight tangle.

He eased me onto the bed, and I couldn't decide whether to laugh or object, so I did both at once. "What are you doing?"

Rick propped his fists on his hips, grinning like a kid who'd just planted the flag on the moon. "Relocating you to the official residence. Didn't want to risk you getting lost in the hallways."

"The official residence?" I tried to sit up, but flopped back, weak with sleep and laughter. "You mean, your room?"

He smirked. "Our room. If you're still willing."

I didn't bother to answer. I just hooked my arm around his neck and dragged him down with me, flattening my body against his, the delicious, impossible weight of him knocking the last of my sleep away. His mouth was warm, insistent, and in seconds I was awake in every cell, hands already snaking under his shirt, greedy for skin.

He made a low sound, somewhere between a growl and a moan, and I gasped into his mouth, the heat of him lighting up every nerve ending in my body. He peeled off his shirt, tossing it to the floor, then skimmed my dress up over my hips and yanked it free, leaving me in nothing but panties and the bralette I'd thrown on that morning. He paused, eyes hungry, then ran his hands over my ribs like he was mapping new territory, every inch worshipful.

"God, you're so fucking beautiful," he said, voice thick. "You know that, right? I'm never getting over you."

I grinned, high on his want. "You better not," I said, grinding up against the hard length of him through his jeans. "Because I've got plans for you, Patrick Daniels. Nasty, unspeakable plans."

He laughed, a raw, feral sound, and bit at my neck, gently, just enough to mark. "Yeah?" he rumbled. "You gonna show me how glad you are to be my roommate?"

"Try and stop me," I breathed, and rolled us, using the element of surprise and the fact that he never expected a woman half his size to move him. He landed with a delicious *oomph*, and for a second I just straddled him, enjoying the view: his arms up, biceps flexed, chest dusted with gold, and that untamed, starving look in his eyes that made me feel dangerous.

I leaned over him, hair curtaining around our faces, and bit his lower lip just shy of hard. "What do you want?" I whispered, all mock-innocence. "You want to fuck me, Rick?" I rocked my hips over him, grinding through the thin cotton of my underwear and his jeans until I felt the zipper dig, maddening and perfect. "You want to put that monster cock inside me and fill me up until I can't even remember my own name?"

He groaned, the sound somewhere between grateful and desperate, and I felt his cock jolt under me, straining the denim. "Yeah," he said, voice raw. "I want to fuck you. I want to bend you over this bed and make you scream my name until the whole goddamn block knows who you belong to."

The words went straight through me, turning every muscle to water. "You think you can handle me?" I shot back, but my voice had already gone ragged, every breath a staccato pulse of want.

He raked his hands up my thighs, thumbs grazing the crease where hips met pelvis, and yanked me forward until my knees boxed his ribs. "Try me," he dared, and I did—I ground down hard, the friction sharp and just this side of brutal, and his head went back, a shiver running through his whole body.

I arched over him, letting my bra slip down off my shoulder, and his hand slipped up to cup my breast, palm rough and hot. He thumbed the nipple through the mesh, then bent to suck it through the lace, tongue circling slow, then biting down just enough to make me gasp. My hips were already rocking, need throbbing between my legs.

"Take off your pants," I demanded, and Rick obeyed, one-handed, shoving them down over his ass while never letting my nipple leave his mouth. I wriggled out of my panties, tossing them aside, and reached for his cock, thick and leaking, the head already flushed almost purple.

I stroked him, slow at first, then tighter, loving the way his whole body bucked, needy and eager. "God, you're so fucking hard for me," I murmured, stroking him root to tip.

He groaned, hands flexing on my hips. "I want to fuck you so hard you see stars. I want you to come on my cock while I'm still buried so deep you can't get away." He gripped my thighs, fingers digging in, and I ground down, pumping him until the base of him slicked with me, slippery and insane.

"Do it," I taunted, lining him up and letting the tip just barely press at my entrance, teasing myself as much as him. "Show me what happens when you fuck me so hard all I remember is you."

His patience snapped—he thrust up in one savage motion, making me cry out. The stretch of him was perfect, obscene, every inch taking me apart and slamming me back together. I clenched down, riding him, using the leverage of his chest and my own hunger to piston up and down, taking all of him, letting him rut up inside until I felt it in my teeth.

He grabbed my ass in both hands, squeezing and spreading me until I opened for him, then fucked up into me with savage rhythm, all restraint gone. I rode him, bracing my hands on his chest, letting my head fall back and my hair whip around my shoulders. He started thrusting so hard I nearly lost my balance, gasping as he bottomed out again and again, the angle hitting some impossible place that made me see white.

"Fuck, you're tight," he gritted, eyes wild, sweat sheening his brow. "You were made for this, made for me. You feel that, Lea?" He slammed up again, making me yelp, then laugh, then yelp again, the pleasure so sharp it almost hurt.

"I feel everything," I groaned, clawing red lines down his chest. "You're too much, Rick, I—"

He cut me off with a palm across the back of my head, dragging me down to kiss him, his lips brutal and perfect, tongue plunging in time with the snap of his hips. I shuddered, every muscle seizing as the heat built, faster and meaner than before. I wanted to see him lose it, wanted to break him open with how desperate I was.

I pressed my mouth to his ear and spat the words: "Come inside me. Get me so full I leak for a week. You wanna see me beg, Rick? Make me beg."

He lost it. He fucked me harder than I thought possible, the wet slap of skin obscene in the quiet, the headboard thumping a counterpoint to his ragged gasp. My orgasm hit with a violence that startled me—I screamed, no words, just raw want, and I spasmed around him so hard it forced a desperate, animal groan from his throat. He came in me, hot and huge, hips jerking as he emptied out, the pleasure so blinding it nearly blacked out his eyes for a second. I stayed on him, milking every last pulse, locked together by the heat and the sweat and the mess.

When I finally slumped forward, limp and throbbing, he wrapped me up in his arms, rolled us to our sides, and held me so tight I thought he'd never let go. I could feel his cock still twitching inside me, the rest of him trembling with effort. I kissed him, slow and lazy, then nuzzled into his neck and let the aftershocks roll through us both.

"Jesus Christ," he panted, voice hoarse and reverent.

I grinned, smug and satisfied. "Admit it. I broke you."

He laughed, low and full, chest rumbling under my cheek. "You did. Congratulations. I am a shell of a minotaur."

"Good."

I curled around him, calf hooked over his thigh, our bodies glued together by sweat and all kinds of other fluids. For a long time, neither of us said anything. The quiet wasn't heavy. It was more like the air after a thunderstorm—clean, a little shocked, but full of that ozone glow that makes you think maybe the world can start over, even if only for an hour.

We stayed tangled, the rhythm of our breaths stretching out until the adrenaline faded and something sweet and drowsy took its place. The room was a shambles—sheets on the floor, a bra slung across the lamp, the air thick with the smell of skin and sex and the lingering afterglow of every wild thing we'd just said and done to each other.

Rick's hand moved slow over my back, tracing lazy circles like he was drawing a map of every freckle, every scar. "So about that giant open space," he said, voice low and teasing. "You know the wall between the shops is load bearing?"

I laughed into his chest, the rumble of it moving through both of us. "That's the first thing you thought of?"

He kissed my temple. "It's the first thing I always think of. That I'm not just building my life around you—I'm building walls and floors and infrastructure, making sure nobody's ever going to take it away." He tipped my chin up and smiled, the curve of it soft and feral at the same time. "I want to build the whole world around you, Azalea. That's the point."

I nipped his collarbone, greedy for his taste. "Then let's do it. Tomorrow. Let's cobble this insanity together before either of us loses our nerve."

He seemed to understand, nodding with a gravity that made my chest tight and sweet. "I'll talk to Randy first thing in the morning." Then, quieter, with a note of awe: "We're really doing this."

"We're really doing this." I sealed it with a kiss, slow and deep, and when we finally drifted into sleep, it was the first time I'd ever fallen asleep with someone and knew for certain I wouldn't wake up alone.

Thank you for Reading!

WRITING SCREWED BY THE Minotaur was a such a joy. I loved writing in the world of Hallow's Cove. Thank you to all the authors who brought this world to life. If you're looking for more Lea and Rick, get the bonus epilogue here!

This book was written during a time of huge change for me and I was kept sane and afloat by my lovely husband, who cheers me on and convinces me I am capable of far more than I think. Thank you for always believing in me.

My two sensitivity readers provided me with such insight and guidance. Without them, Lea wouldn't be the character she is. Thank you so much, Stephanie and Cambria, for sharing your wisdom and lived experience. Your advice was invaluable!

Huge thank you to my editors Alex and Emily, you make me so much more confident in putting out books. It is a pleasure to work with both of you.

Finally, to my group of author friends who hold my hand whenever I have to do something big and scary, thank you for pushing me to try something outside my comfort zone. I wouldn't be where I am without you.

Hallow's Cove

Looking for more adventures in Hallow's Cove? Here are the next books in the series...

Also by Jenifer Wood

Abandoned on Niflheim

Agnarr's Teacher
Agnarr's Jarlin
Steve's Barmaid
Fenrik's Fate

About the Author

JEN HAS BEEN READING for as long as she can remember. She used to get in trouble for reading Little House on the Prairie under her desk in elementary school. Jen's day job is advocating for adolescent mental health, something she doesn't see giving up any time soon.

Jen is married to a very polite Englishman she brought back as a souvenir from her college study abroad trip. She has identical twin mutants who make her question her sanity daily. She enjoys reading about alien peens, napping, and watching soothing cooking shows.

She is a goth kid at heart and truly wishes she could wear platform combat boots and black nail polish on all occasions.

www.authorjeniferwood.com